BOOK NUMBER J9162

NAME of PUPIL	ROOM NUMBER	DATE ISSUED	DATE RETURNED
Gretila Walker	124	2/6/65	
Steven	124	4/15/67	
Jean Williams	121	3/5/68	
Alma La Rue	A 267	5/1/68	
Bob Ray	004	Feb, 16, 1970	

11/6/64

The
Call
of the
Wild

by Jack London

edited by

Mary Yost Sandrus

Scott, Foresman and Company

Chicago, Atlanta, Dallas, Palo Alto, Fair Lawn, N. J.

Designed by Marita Robinson

Illustrated by Leon Bishop

Contents

1

Kidnaped

Buck did not read the newspapers. Otherwise he would have known that trouble was coming, not only for himself, but for every dog, strong of muscle and with warm, long hair. Because men, groping in the arctic darkness, had found gold, and thousands of them were rushing into the Northland. These men wanted dogs, heavy dogs, with strong muscles and furry coats to protect them from the frost.

Buck lived at a big house in California's sun-kissed Santa Clara Valley. Judge Miller's place it was called. It stood back from the road, half hidden among the trees. A wide, cool porch ran around its four sides. Driveways wound about through wide lawns to the house under the tall poplar trees. At the rear were great stables and a dozen or more stable boys. There were rows and rows of grapes, green pastures, orchards, and berry patches. Then there was the pumping plant for the well and the big cement tank where Judge Miller's boys swam.

And over all this Buck ruled. Here he was born, and here he had lived the four years of his life. It was true, there were other dogs, but they did not count. They came and went, lived in kennels, or in the house. Toots, the Japanese pug, or Ysabel, the Mexican hairless, rarely put nose out of doors or set foot to ground. In the kennels there were twenty fox terriers.

But Buck was neither house dog nor kennel dog. The whole realm was his. He plunged into the swimming tank or went hunting with the Judge's sons. He went with Mollie and Alice, the Judge's daughters, on long evening or early morning walks. On wintry nights he lay at the Judge's feet before the roaring library fire. He let the Judge's grandsons ride on his back, or rolled them in the grass. He guarded their footsteps through wild adventures down to the fountain in the stable yard, and as far as the berry patches. Among the terriers he strutted and Toots and Ysabel he ignored. For he was king—king over all creeping, crawling, flying things of Judge Miller's place, humans included.

His father, Elmo, a huge St. Bernard, had been the Judge's companion, and Buck would surely follow in the way of his father. Buck was not so large—he weighed only one hundred forty pounds—for his mother, Shep, had been a Scotch shepherd dog. During the four years since his puppyhood he had lived well. He had a fine pride in himself like a country gentleman. But he had saved himself by not becoming a mere pampered house dog. Hunting and kindred outdoor delights had kept down the fat and hardened his muscles.

This was Buck in the fall of 1897, when the Klondike gold strike dragged men from all the world into the frozen North. But Buck did not read the newspapers, and he did not know that Manuel, one of the gardener's helpers, was no friend. Manuel needed money. The wages of a gardener's helper do not take care of the needs of a wife and numerous children. Besides, Manuel loved to gamble. And gambling requires lots of money.

The Judge was at a meeting and the boys were at their club, on the night Manuel took Buck. No one saw him and Buck go off through the orchard on what Buck imagined was merely a stroll. Only one saw them arrive at the little flag station known as College Park. This man talked with Manuel, and gave him money.

"You might wrap up the goods before you deliver them," the stranger said gruffly.

Manuel doubled a piece of rope around Buck's neck under the collar.

"Twist it, and you'll choke him plenty," said Manuel.

Buck had accepted the rope quietly. He had learned to trust men he knew, and to give them credit for a wisdom that outreached his own. But when the ends of the rope were placed in the stranger's hands, Buck growled. He was displeased.

But to his surprise the rope tightened around his neck, shutting off his breath. In quick rage he sprang at the man, who met him halfway and caught him close by the throat. With a twist the man threw Buck over on his back. Then the rope tightened mercilessly, while Buck struggled in a fury, his tongue lolling out of his mouth and his great chest panting.

11

Never in all his life had he been so vilely treated and never in all his life had he been so angry. But he lost strength, his eyes glazed, and he knew nothing when the train was flagged. The two men threw him into the baggage car.

The next he knew his tongue was hurting and he was being jolted along in some kind of car. The hoarse shriek of a locomotive whistling at a crossing told him where he was. He had traveled too often with the Judge not to know that he was riding in a baggage car.

When they stopped, he opened his eyes, and into them came the unbridled anger of a kidnaped king. The man sprang for Buck's throat, but Buck was too quick for him. His jaws closed on the hand until his senses were choked out of him once more.

"Yep, has fits," the man said, hiding his bloody hand from the baggageman, who had been attracted by the sounds of struggle.

"I'm taking him up for the boss to San

Francisco. A dog doctor there thinks that he can cure him."

Concerning that night's ride, the man talked in a little shed on the San Francisco water front.

"All I get is fifty dollars for it," he grumbled. "And I wouldn't do it over for a thousand."

His hand was wrapped in a bloody handkerchief, and his right trouser leg was ripped from knee to ankle.

"How much did the other fellow get?" he was asked.

"A hundred," was the reply. "Wouldn't take less, so help me."

"That makes a hundred fifty," the other man said, "and he's worth it, or I'm a squarehead."

The kidnaper undid the bloody wrappings and looked at his hand. "If I don't get the hydrophoby—"

"It'll be because you were born to hang,"

13

laughed the other. "Here, lend me a hand."

Dazed, suffering intolerable pain from throat and tongue, with the life half throttled out of him, Buck attempted to face the men. But he was thrown down and choked repeatedly, till they succeeded in filing the heavy brass collar from his neck. Then the rope was removed, and he was flung into a cagelike crate.

There he lay for the remainder of the weary night, nursing his wrath and wounded pride. He could not understand what it all meant. What did they want with him, these strange men? Why were they keeping him penned up in this narrow crate? He sprang to his feet every time the shed door rattled open, expecting to see the Judge, or the boys at least. But each time it was the same man that peered in at him by the sickly light of a candle. And each time the joyful bark that trembled in Buck's throat was twisted into a savage growl.

In the morning four men entered and picked

up the crate. They were evil-looking creatures, ragged and dirty. Buck stormed and
raged at them through the bars. They only
laughed and poked sticks at him, which he
promptly grabbed with his teeth till he realized that that was what they wanted. Then he
lay down crossly and allowed the crate to be
lifted into a wagon. He and the crate then began a passage through many hands. Clerks in
the express office took charge of him and he
was carted about in another wagon. A truck
carried him, with many boxes and parcels,
upon a ferry steamer. He was trucked off the
steamer into a great railway depot, and finally
deposited in an express car.

For two days and nights this express car was
dragged along at the tail of shrieking loco-
motives. And for two days and nights Buck
neither ate nor drank. In his anger he had met
the first advances of the express messengers
with growls, and they had teased him. When
he flung himself against the bars, quivering,

they laughed at him and taunted him. They growled and barked like dogs, mewed, flapped their arms, and crowed. It was all very silly, he knew, and he became angrier and angrier. He did not mind the hunger so much, but the lack of water caused him severe suffering.

He was glad for one thing: the rope was off his neck. That had given them an unfair advantage. Now that it was off, he would show them. They would never get another rope around his neck. He was sure of that. For two days and nights he neither ate nor drank. And during those two days and nights of torment, his eyes turned bloodshot, and he became a raging fiend. So changed was he that the Judge himself would not have recognized him. The express messengers breathed with relief when they bundled him off the train at Seattle.

2

A Lesson

Four men carried the crate from the wagon into a small, high-walled back yard. A stout man, with a red sweater that sagged at the neck, came out and signed the book for the driver. That man Buck thought was to be his next tormentor, and he hurled himself savagely against the bars. The man smiled grimly, and brought a hatchet and a club.

"You ain't going to take him out now?" the driver asked. "Sure," the man replied, driving the hatchet into the crate to pry it open.

There was an instantaneous scattering of the four men who had carried in the crate. From safe perches on top the wall they prepared to watch the performance.

Buck rushed at the splintering wood, sinking his teeth into it. Wherever the hatchet fell on the outside, he was there on the inside, snarling and growling. He was as furiously anxious to get out as the man in the red sweater was calmly intent on getting him out.

"Now, you red-eyed devil," the man said, when he had made an opening sufficient for the passage of Buck's body. At the same time he dropped the hatchet and shifted the club to his right hand.

And Buck was truly a red-eyed devil, as he drew himself together for the spring. His hair was bristling, his mouth foaming, and there was a mad glitter in his bloodshot eyes. Straight at the man he launched his one hundred forty pounds of fury. In midair, just as his jaws were about to close on the man, he

received a shock that checked his body and brought his teeth together with an agonizing clip. He whirled over, with the ground first on his back and then on his side. He had never been struck by a club in his life, and did not understand. With a snarl that was part bark and more scream, he was again on his feet and launched into the air. Again the shock came and he was brought crushingly to the ground. This time he was aware that it was the club, but his madness knew no caution. A dozen times he charged, and as often the club broke the charge and smashed him down.

After a particularly fierce blow he crawled to his feet, too dazed to rush. He staggered limply about, the blood flowing from nose and mouth and ears, his beautiful coat sprayed and spotted with blood. Then the man advanced and dealt him a frightful blow on the nose. All the pain he had endured was as nothing compared with this. With a roar that was almost lion-like, he again hurled himself at the man.

But the man coolly caught him by the under-jaw, at the same time wrenching downward and backward. Buck described a complete circle in the air, and half of another, then crashed to the ground on his head and chest.

Then he rushed for the last time. The man struck the shrewd blow he had purposely withheld for so long and Buck went down, knocked utterly senseless.

"He's no slouch at dog-breaking, that's what I say," one of the men on the wall cried.

"I'd rather break ponies any day, and twice on Sundays," was the reply of the driver. He climbed on the wagon and started the horses.

Buck's senses came back to him, but not his strength. He lay where he had fallen, and from there he watched the man in the red sweater.

"Answers to the name of Buck," the man said, reading a letter which had come with the crate and contents. "Well, Buck, my boy," he went on, "we've had our little row, and the best thing we can do is to let it go at that. You've learned your place, and I know mine. Be a good dog, and all will go well. Be a bad dog, and I'll whale the stuffing out of you. Understand?"

As he spoke he fearlessly patted the head he had so mercilessly pounded. Though Buck's hair rose at the touch of the hand, he endured it without protest. When the man brought water he drank eagerly, and later bolted a generous meal of raw meat, chunk by chunk, from the man's hand.

He was beaten, he knew, but he was not broken. He saw, once for all, that he stood no chance against a man with a club. He had learned a lesson, and in all his life he never forgot it. That club was his introduction to the reign of savage law, and he met the introduction halfway.

The facts of life began to take on a fiercer look. While he faced that fact uncowed, he faced it with all the aroused cunning of his nature.

22

As the days went by, other dogs came in crates and at the ends of ropes, some quietly, and some raging and roaring as he had come. One and all, he watched them pass under the control of the man in the red sweater. Again and again, as he looked at each brutal performance, the lesson was driven home to Buck. A man with a club was a lawgiver, a master to be obeyed, though not necessarily to be won over.

Of this last Buck at least was never guilty. Though he did see beaten dogs that fawned upon the man, and wagged their tails, and licked his hand. Also he saw one dog, that would neither be won over nor obey, finally killed in the struggle for mastery.

Now and again men came, strangers, who talked excitedly, pleadingly, and in all kinds of fashions to the man in the red sweater. And when money passed between them the strangers took one or more of the dogs away with them. Buck wondered where they went, for they never came back. But fear of the future was strong upon him, and he was glad each time when he was not selected.

Yet his time came. One day a little dried-up man arrived who spoke broken English and many strange words which Buck could not understand.

"That one bully dog," he cried, when his eyes lit upon Buck. "Eh? How much?"

"Three hundred, and a present at that," was the prompt reply of the man in the red sweater. "And seeing it's government money, you've got no kick coming, eh, Perrault?"

Perrault grinned. Considering that the price of dogs had been boomed skyward by the demand, it was not an unfair sum for so fine an animal. The Canadian government would be no loser, nor would its dispatches travel the slower. Perrault knew dogs. Buck looked as if he was one in a thousand—"One in ten thousand," Perrault thought.

Buck saw money pass between them, and

was not surprised when Curly, a good-natured Newfoundland, and he were led away by the little dried-up man. That was the last he saw of the man in the red sweater, and as Curly and he looked at Seattle from the deck of the ship *Narwhal,* it was the last he saw of the warm Southland.

Curly and he were taken below by Perrault and turned over to a giant called Francois.

Perrault was half French-Canadian and half Indian, a half-breed. They were a new kind of men to Buck, but he was destined to see many more like them. While he developed no love for them, he grew honestly to respect them. He speedily learned that Perrault and Francois were fair, just men, and too wise in the ways of dogs to be fooled by dogs.

In the 'tween-decks of the ship, Buck and Curly joined two other dogs. One of them was a big, snow-white fellow from Spitsbergen who had been brought away by a whaling captain. Spitz was friendly, in a sly sort of way, smiling into one's face while he planned some trick. For instance, he stole Buck's food at the first meal. As Buck sprang to punish him Francois' whip sang through the air, reaching the other dog first. Nothing remained to Buck but to recover the bone. That was fair of Francois, and Buck respected the half-breed.

The other dog made no advances, nor received any. And he did not attempt to steal from the newcomers. He was a gloomy fellow, and he showed Curly plainly that all he desired was to be left alone. And further, that there would be trouble if he were not left alone. He was called "Dave." He ate and slept, or yawned between times, and took interest in nothing. When the ship crossed Queen Charlotte Sound and rolled and pitched and bucked like a thing possessed, Buck and Curly grew excited. They were half wild with fear. Dave raised his head as though annoyed at them, yawned, and went to sleep again.

Day and night the ship throbbed to the pulse

of the propeller. One day was very like another, but Buck knew that the weather was steadily growing colder. At last, one morning, the propeller was quiet, and there seemed to be excitement. Buck felt it, as did the other dogs, and knew that a change was at hand. Soon Francois leashed them and brought them on deck.

At the first step upon the cold surface, Buck's feet sank into a white mushy something very like mud. He sprang back with a snort. More of this white stuff was falling through the air. He shook himself, but more of it fell upon him. He sniffed it curiously, then licked some up on his tongue. It bit like fire, and the next instant was gone. This puzzled him. He tried it again, with the same result. The onlookers laughed uproariously, and Buck felt ashamed, he knew not why, for it was his first snow.

Buck's first day on the Dyea beach was a nightmare. Every hour was filled with shock

and surprise. He had been suddenly jerked
from the heart of civilization and flung into
the heart of things uncivilized. No lazy, sun-
kissed life was this, with nothing to do but
loaf. Here was neither peace, nor rest, nor a
moment's safety. All was confusion and action, and every moment life and limb were in
peril. There was need to be constantly alert.

3

The Fight

These dogs and men were not town dogs and men. They were savages, all of them, who knew no law but the law of club and fang.

He had never seen dogs fight as these wolf-ish creatures fought, and his first experience taught him an unforgettable lesson. It is true it was another's experience, else he would not have lived to profit by it. Curly was the victim.

They were camped near the log store, where she, in her friendly way, made advances to a Husky dog. He was the size of a full-grown wolf, though not half so large as she. There was no warning, only a leap in like a flash, a metallic clip of teeth, a leap out equally swift, and Curly's face was ripped open from eye to jaw.

It was the wolf manner of fighting, to strike and leap away, but there was more to it than this. Thirty or forty Huskies ran to the spot and surrounded the fighters in an intent and silent circle. Buck did not understand that silence nor the eager way with which they were licking their chops. Curly rushed the Husky who struck again and leaped aside. He met her next rush with his chest, and tumbled her off her feet. She never regained them. This was what the onlooking Huskies had waited for. They closed in upon her, snarling and yelping, and she was buried, screaming with agony, beneath the bristling mass of bodies.

30

So sudden was it, and so unexpected, that Buck was taken aback. He saw Spitz run out his scarlet tongue in a way he had of laughing. Then Buck saw Francois swinging an ax, spring into the mess of dogs. Three men with clubs were helping him scatter them. It did not take long. Two minutes from the time Curly went down, the last of the Huskies were clubbed off. But she lay there limp and lifeless in the bloody, trampled snow, almost torn to pieces. Francois was standing over her and cursing horribly.

The scene often came back to Buck to trouble him in his sleep. So that was the way. No fair play. Once down, that was the end of you. Well, he would see to it that he never went down. Spitz ran out his tongue and laughed again, and from that moment Buck hated him with a bitter and deathless hatred.

Before he had recovered from the first shock caused by the death of Curly, he received another shock. Francois fastened upon him an

arrangement of straps and buckles. It was a harness, such as he had seen the boys put on the horses at home. As he had seen horses work, so he was set to work. He hauled Francois on a sled to the forest that fringed the valley, and returned with a load of firewood.

Though his dignity was sorely hurt by being made a work animal, he was too wise to refuse. He buckled down with a will and did his best, though it was all new and strange. Francois was stern, demanding instant obedience, and with his whip receiving instant obedience. Dave, who was an experienced wheeler, nipped Buck's hindquarters whenever Buck was in error. Spitz was the leader, and likewise experienced. He could not always get at Buck, but he growled sharp reproof now and again. Or he cunningly threw his weight in the harness straps to jerk Buck into the way he should go.

Buck learned easily, and under the combined tuition of his two mates and Francois made remarkable progress. Before they re-

33

turned to camp he knew enough to stop at "ho," to go ahead at "mush," to swing wide on the bends, and to keep clear of the wheeler when the loaded sled shot downhill at their heels.

"Three very good dogs," Francois told Perrault. "That Buck, I teach him quick as anything."

By afternoon, Perrault, who was in a hurry to be on the trail with his dispatches, returned with two more dogs. "Billee" and "Joe" he called them, two brothers, and true Huskies both. Sons of the one mother though they were, they were as different as day and night. Billee's one fault was his good nature, while Joe was the very opposite, disagreeable with a perpetual snarl and an evil eye.

Buck received them in a comradely fashion. Dave ignored them, while Spitz proceeded to thrash first one and then the other. Billee wagged his tail appeasingly and turned to run when he saw that appeasement was no good.

He cried (still appeasingly) when Spitz' sharp teeth scored his flank.

But no matter how Spitz circled, Joe whirled around on his heels to face him, mane bristling, ears laid back, lips snarling. His jaws clipped together as fast as he could snap, and his eyes gleamed devilishly. So terrible was Joe's appearance that Spitz was forced to quit. To cover his own discomfiture he turned upon the wailing Billee and drove him into camp.

By evening Perrault secured another dog, an old Husky, long and lean, with a battle-scarred face and only one eye which flashed a warning and that commanded respect. He was called Sol-leks, which means the Angry One. Like Dave, he asked nothing, gave nothing, expected nothing. When he marched slowly and deliberately into their midst, he was left alone even by Spitz. Buck was unlucky enough to discover Sol-leks' one peculiarity. He did not like to be approached on his blind side. Of this offense Buck was unwittingly guilty. Sol-leks whirled upon him and slashed his shoulder to the bone for three inches up and down. Forever after Buck avoided Sol-leks' blind side, and had no more trouble.

That night Buck faced the great problem of sleeping. The tent, lit by a candle, glowed warmly in the midst of the white snow. When he, as a matter of course, entered it, both Perrault and Francois threw cooking utensils at him. He recovered and fled into the outer cold. A chill wind was blowing that nipped him sharply and bit into his wounded shoulder. He lay down on the snow and attempted to sleep, but the frost soon drove him shivering to his feet.

Miserable, he wandered about among the many tents, only to find that one place was as cold as another. Here and there savage dogs rushed upon him, but he bristled his neck hair and snarled, for he was learning fast, and they let him go his way.

Finally an idea came to him. He would return and see how his own teammates were making out. To his astonishment, they had disappeared. Again he wandered about through the great camp, looking for them, and again he returned. Were they in the tent? No, that could not be, else he would not have been driven out. Then where could they possibly be?

With drooping tail and shivering body, very forlorn indeed, he aimlessly circled the tent. Suddenly the snow gave way beneath his fore-legs and he sank down. Something wriggled under his feet. He sprang back, bristling and snarling, fearful of the unseen and unknown. But a friendly little yelp reassured him, and he went back to look. A whiff of warm air reached to his nostrils, and there, curled up under the snow in a snug ball, lay Billee. He whined, squirmed, and wriggled to show his good will, and even tried to lick Buck's face with his warm, wet tongue.

Another lesson. So that was the way they did it, eh? Buck selected a spot, and with much fuss and waste effort proceeded to dig a hole for himself. In a moment the heat from his body filled the space and he was asleep. The day had been long and he slept soundly and comfortably, though he growled and barked and wrestled with bad dreams.

Nor did he open his eyes till roused by the noises of the waking camp. At first he did not know where he was. It had snowed during the night and he was completely buried. The snow walls pressed him on every side, and a great fear swept through him—the fear of the wild thing for the trap. It was instinct that caused the fear, and not his own experience. The muscles of his whole body contracted. The hair on his neck and shoulders stood on end, and with a ferocious snarl he bounded straight up into the blinding day. The snow flew about him in a flashing cloud.

Before he landed on his feet, he saw the white camp spread out before him and knew where he was. He remembered all that had

passed from the time he went for a stroll with Manuel to the hole he had dug for himself the night before.

A shout from Francois hailed his appearance. "What I say?" the dog driver cried to Perrault. "That Buck for sure learn quick as anything."

Perrault nodded gravely. As messenger for the Canadian government, bearing important dispatches, he was anxious to secure the best dogs, and he was particularly gladdened by the possession of Buck.

4

Straps

Three more Huskies were added to the team inside an hour, making a total of nine. Before another quarter of an hour had passed they were in harness and swinging up the trail toward the Dyea Canyon. Buck was glad to be gone, and though the work was hard he found he did not particularly despise it. He was surprised at the eagerness of the whole team which he could feel. Still more surprising was the change in Dave and Sol-leks. They were new dogs, utterly transformed by the harness.

All passiveness and unconcern had dropped from them. They were alert and active, anxious that the work should go well, and fiercely irritable with whatever, by delay or confusion, retarded that work. The toil of the harness seemed all that they lived for, and the only thing in which they took delight.

Dave was wheeler or sled dog, pulling in front of him was Buck, then came Sol-leks. The rest of the team was strung out ahead, single file, to the leader, which position was filled by Spitz.

Buck had been purposely placed between Dave and Sol-leks so that he might receive instruction. Quick pupil that he was, they were equally good teachers, never allowing him to make mistakes and helping their teaching with their sharp teeth. + start

Dave was fair and very wise. He never nipped Buck without cause, and he never failed to nip him when he stood in need of it. As Francois' whip backed Dave up, Buck found it to be cheaper to mend his ways than to get even. Once, during a brief halt, when Buck got tangled in the harness straps and delayed the start, both Dave and Sol-leks flew at him and gave him a sound beating. The resulting tangle was even worse, but after that Buck took good care to keep the straps clear. When the day was done, he had mastered his work well. Francois' whip snapped less frequently, and Perrault even honored Buck by lifting up his feet and carefully examining them.

It was a hard day's run, up the Canyon, through Sheep Camp, past the Scales and the timber line. They went across glaciers and snowdrifts hundreds of feet deep, and over the great Chilcoot Pass. It stands between the salt water and the fresh and guards forbiddingly the sad and lonely North. They made good time down the chain of lakes which fills the craters of inactive volcanoes. Late that night they pulled into the huge camp at the head of Lake Bennett. There thousands of gold seekers were building boats before the break-up of the ice in the spring.

Buck made his hole in the snow and slept. All too early he was jerked out in the cold darkness and harnessed with his mates to the sled.

That day they made forty miles, because the snow on the trail was packed hard. The next day, and for many days to follow, they broke their own trail, worked harder, and made poorer time. As a rule, Perrault traveled ahead of the team, packing the snow with snowshoes to make it easier for them. Francois, guiding the sled at the gee pole, sometimes exchanged places with him, but not often. Perrault was in a hurry, and he prided himself on his knowledge of ice, which was important. The fall ice was very thin, and where there was swift water, there was no ice at all.

Day after day, for days unending, Buck toiled in the harness. Always they broke camp in the dark, and the first gray of dawn found them hitting the trail with fresh miles behind them. And always they pitched camp after dark, eating their bit of fish, and crawling to sleep into the snow. Buck was ravenous. The pound and a half of sun-dried salmon, which was his ration for each day, seemed to be nothing. He never had enough, and always suffered from hunger. The other dogs, because they weighed less and were born to the life, received only a pound of fish and managed to keep in good condition. Buck swiftly lost the habits of his old life. He had been a dainty eater. Now he found that his mates, finishing first robbed him of his unfinished ration. There was no defending it. While he was fighting off two or three, the food was disappearing down the throats of the others. Buck began to eat as fast as they. And he was so hungry that he was not above taking what did not belong to him. He watched and learned. One day he saw Pike, one of the new dogs, a clever loafer and thief, slyly steal a slice of bacon when Perrault's back was turned. Buck did the same the following day, getting away with the whole chunk. A great uproar was raised, but he was unsuspected. Dub, an awkward blunderer who was always getting caught, was punished for Buck's misdeed.

This marked Buck as able to live in the Northland. It marked his ability to adjust himself to changing conditions, which could mean swift and terrible death. It marked, further, the decay or going to pieces of his moral nature, a vain thing and a handicap in the ruthless struggle for existence. It was well enough in the Southland, under the law of love and fellowship, to respect private property and personal feelings. In the Northland, under the law of club and fang, whoever took such things into account was a fool.

Not that Buck reasoned it out. He was fit, that was all, and unconsciously he adjusted himself to the new way of life. All his days, no matter what the odds, he had never run from a fight. But the club of the man in the red sweater had beaten into him a more uncivilized code. Civilized, he could have died for a cause, say to guard Judge Miller's riding whip. But now he would flee to save his hide. He did not steal for joy of it, but because of the hunger of his stomach. He did not rob openly, but stole secretly and cunningly, out of respect for club and fang. In short, the things he did were done because it was easier to do them than not to do them.

His uncivilized development was rapid. His muscles became hard as iron and he grew used to all ordinary pain. He could eat anything, no matter how bad or indigestible. And, once eaten he was able to make use of it. His sight and scent became remarkably keen, while his hearing developed even more. In his sleep he could hear the faintest sound and know whether or not it meant peace or peril. He learned to bite the ice out with his teeth when

47

it collected between his toes. When he was thirsty and there was a thick scum of ice over the water hole, he would break it by rearing and striking it with stiff forelegs. He had the ability to scent the wind and forecast it a night in advance. No matter how breathless the air when he dug his nest by tree or bank, the wind that later blew inevitably found him away from it, sheltered and snug.

And not only did he learn by experience, but instincts long dead became alive again. The wild dogs used to run in packs through the forest and killed their meat as they ran it down. It was no task for him to learn to fight with cut and slash and the quick wolf snap. In this manner his forgotten ancestors had fought. They quickened the old life within him, and the old tricks which they had stamped into the breed were his tricks. They came to him without effort or discovery, as though they had been his always. On the still, cold nights, he pointed his nose at a star and howled long and

wolflike. It was his forefathers, dead and dust, pointing nose at star and howling down through the centuries and through him. And he voiced their woe and what to them was the meaning of the stillness, and the cold, and the dark.

5

Wolflike

The wolflike beast was strong in Buck, and under the fierce conditions of trail life it grew and grew. Yet it was a secret growth. His new cunning gave him poise and control. He was too busy adjusting himself to the new life to feel at ease, and not only did he not pick fights, but he avoided them whenever possible.

On the other hand, Spitz never lost an opportunity of showing his teeth, possibly because he saw in Buck a dangerous rival. He even went out of his way to bully Buck, trying constantly to start the fight which could end only in the death of one or the other.

Early in the trip this might have taken place had it not been for an accident. At the end of this day they made a miserable camp on the shore of Lake Lebarge. Driving snow, a wind that cut like a white-hot knife, and darkness had forced them to grope for a camping place. They could hardly have fared worse. At their backs rose a straight wall of rock, and Perrault and Francois had to make their fire and spread their sleeping robes on the ice of the lake itself. They had left the tent at Dyea in order to travel lightly. A few sticks of driftwood furnished them with a fire that thawed down through the ice and left them to eat supper in the dark.

Close in under the sheltering rock Buck made his nest. So snug and warm was it, that he was unwilling to leave it when Francois passed around the fish which he had first thawed over the fire. But when Buck finished his ration and returned, he found his nest occupied. A warning snarl told him that the occupant was Spitz. Till now Buck had avoided trouble with his enemy, but this was too much. The beast in him roared. He sprang upon Spitz with a fury which surprised them both. Spitz was surprised, for his whole experience with Buck had gone to teach him that his rival was an unusually timid dog. Buck managed to hold his own only because of his great weight and size.

Francois was surprised, too, when they shot out in a tangle from the nest and he saw the cause of the trouble.

"A-a-ah!" he cried to Buck. "Give it to him! Give it to him, the dirty thief!"

Spitz was equally willing. He was crying with sheer rage as he circled back and forth for a chance to spring in. Buck was no less eager, and no less cautious, as he likewise circled back and forth. But it was then that the unexpected happened. It began with a cry from Perrault, the sound of a club upon a bony frame, and a shrill yelp of pain. The camp was suddenly discovered to be alive with furry forms—starving Huskies, almost a hundred of them, who had scented the camp from some Indian village. They had crept in while Buck and Spitz were fighting, and when the two men sprang among them with stout clubs they showed their teeth and fought back.

They were crazed by the smell of the food. Perrault found one with head buried in the food box. His club landed heavily on the ribs, and the food box was upset on the ground. On the instant a score of the famished brutes were scrambling for the bread and bacon. The clubs fell upon them unheeded. They yelped and howled under the rain of blows, but struggled none the madly till the last crumb had been eaten.

In the meantime the astonished team dogs

had burst out of their nests only to be set upon by the fierce invaders. Never had Buck seen such dogs. It seemed as though their bones would burst through their skins. They were all bones with loosely hung hides, with blazing eyes and dripping fangs. But the hunger-madness made them terrifying. There was no opposing them. The team dogs were swept back against the cliff.

Buck was attacked by three Huskies, and his head and shoulders were ripped and slashed. The din was frightful. Billee was crying as usual. Dave and Sol-leks, dripping blood from their wounds, were fighting bravely side by side. Joe was snapping like a devil. Once, his teeth closed on the foreleg of a Husky, and he crunched down through the bone. Pike, the loafer, leaped upon the crippled animal, breaking its neck.

Buck got a frothing dog by the throat, and was sprayed with blood when his teeth sank through the jugular vein. The warm taste of it in his mouth goaded him to greater fierceness. He flung himself upon another, and at the same time felt teeth sink into his own throat. It was Spitz, attacking from the side.

Perrault and Francois having cleaned out their part of the camp, hurried to save their sled dogs. The wild wave of starving beasts rolled back before them, and Buck shook himself free. But it was only for a moment. The two men were compelled to run back to save the remaining food.

And the Huskies returned to the attack on the team. Billee, terrified into bravery, sprang through the savage circle and fled away over the ice. Pike and Dub followed on his heels, with the rest of the team behind. As Buck drew himself together to spring after them, out of the tail of his eye he saw Spitz rush upon him. Once off his feet and under that mass of Huskies, there would be no hope for him. But he braced himself to the shock of Spitz' charge, then joined the flight out on the lake.

Later, the nine team dogs gathered together and sought shelter in the forest. They were in a sorry plight. There was not one who was not wounded in four or five places, while some were wounded seriously. Dub was badly injured in a hind leg. Dolly, the last Husky added to the team at Dyea, had a badly torn throat. Joe had lost an eye. Billee, the good-natured, with an ear chewed to ribbons, cried and whimpered throughout the night.

At daybreak they limped wearily back to camp, to find the wild dogs gone and the two men in bad tempers. Fully half their food supply was gone. The Huskies had chewed through the sled lashings and canvas coverings. In fact, nothing had escaped them. They had eaten a pair of Perrault's moose-hide moccasins, chunks out of the leather straps, and even two feet of lash from the end of Francois' whip. Francois looked over his wounded dogs.

"Ah, my friends," he said softly, "maybe

57

it make you mad dogs, those many bites. Maybe all the dogs are mad! What you think, Perrault?"

The messenger shook his head. With four hundred miles of trail still between him and Dawson, he could not afford to have madness break out among his dogs. Two hours of work got the harnesses into shape, and the wound-stiffened team was under way. It struggled painfully over the hardest part of the trail they had yet faced, and for that matter, the hardest between them and Dawson.

The Thirty Mile River was wide open. It was only in the quiet places that the ice held at all. Six days of exhausting toil were required to cover those thirty terrible miles. And terrible they were, for every foot of them was traveled at the risk of life to dog and man. A dozen times, Perrault, nosing the way, broke through the ice being saved by the long pole he carried. He held it so that it fell each time across the hole made by his body. But a cold snap

was on. The thermometer registered fifty below zero, and each time he broke through he was compelled for very life to build a fire and dry his clothes.

Nothing stopped him. It was because of this that he had been chosen for government messenger. He took all manner of risks, struggling on from dawn to dark. The ice bent and crackled underfoot, but they dared not halt. Once, the sled broke through, with Dave and Buck, and they were half frozen and all but drowned by the time they were dragged out. The usual fire was necessary to save them. They were coated solidly with ice, and the two men kept them on the run around the fire, sweating and thawing, very close to the flames.

At another time Spitz went through, dragging the whole team after him up to Buck, who strained backward with all his strength, his forepaws on the slippery edge and the ice quivering and snapping all around. But behind him was Dave, likewise straining backward, and behind the sled was Francois, also pulling back.

Again, the rim ice broke away before and behind, and there was no escape except up the cliff. Perrault scaled it by a miracle, while Francois prayed for just that miracle. And with every strap and sled lashing and the last bit of harness drawn into a long rope, the dogs were hoisted, one by one, to the top of the cliff. Francois came up last, after the sled and load. Then came the search for a place to descend. Descent was at last made by the aid of the rope, and night found them back on the river with only a quarter of a mile gained in the whole day.

By the time they made the Hootalinqua River and good ice, Buck was played out. The rest of the dogs were in like condition. But Perrault, to make up lost time, pushed them late and early. The first day they covered thirty-five miles to the Big Salmon River. The next day, they went thirty-five miles more to the Little Salmon River. The third day forty miles, which brought them well up toward the Five Fingers.

Buck's feet were not so hard as the feet of the Huskies. His had softened during the many generations since the day his last wild father was tamed by a cave dweller or river man. All day long he limped in agony, and camp once made, lay down like a dead dog. Hungry as he was, he would not move to receive his ration of fish, which Francois had to bring to him.

Also, the dog driver rubbed Buck's feet for half an hour each night after supper, and sacrificed the tops of his own moccasins to make four moccasins for Buck. This was a great relief, and Buck caused the face of Perrault to twist itself into a grin one morning when Francois forgot the moccasins and Buck lay on his back, his four feet waving appealingly in the air, and refused to budge without the moccasins. Later his feet grew hardened to the trail.

At the Pelly River one morning, as they were harnessing up, Dolly went suddenly mad. She gave a long, heartbreaking wolf howl that sent every dog bristling with fear, then sprang straight for Buck. He had never seen a dog go mad, nor did he have any reason to fear madness. Yet he knew that here was horror, and fled away from it in a panic. Straight away he raced, with Dolly, panting and foaming one leap behind. Nor could she gain on him, so great was his terror, nor could he leave her, so great was her madness. He plunged through the wooded part of the island, fled down to the lower end, crossed a back channel filled with rough ice to another island, gained a third island, curved back to the main river, and started to cross it. And all the time, though he did not look, he could hear her snarling just one leap behind.

Francois called to him a quarter mile away and he doubled back, still one leap ahead, gasping painfully for air and putting all his faith in the hope that Francois would save him. The dog driver held the ax poised in his hand, and as Buck shot past him the ax crashed down upon mad Dolly's head.

Buck staggered over against the sled, exhausted, sobbing for breath, helpless. This was Spitz' opportunity. He sprang upon Buck, and twice his teeth sank and ripped and tore the flesh to the bone. Then Francois' lash descended, and Buck had the satisfaction of watching Spitz receive the worst whipping as yet administered to any of the team.

"One devil, that Spitz," remarked Perrault. "Someday he'll kill that Buck."

"That Buck two devils," was Francois' reply. "All the time I watch that Buck I know for sure. Some fine day he'll get mad and then he'll chew that Spitz all up and spit him out on the snow. Sure. I know."

6

War

From then on it was war between them. Spitz, as lead dog and master of the team, felt his position threatened by this strange Southland dog. And strange Buck was to him, for of the many Southland dogs he had known, not one had shown up well in camp and on trail. They were all too soft, dying under the toil, the frost, and starvation. Buck was the exception. He alone endured, matching the Husky in strength, savagery, and cunning. Then he was a masterful dog, and what made him dangerous was the fact that the club of the man in the red sweater had knocked all blind caring out of his desire for mastery. He was cunning, and could bide his time with patience.

The clash for leadership would come. Buck wanted it. He wanted it because it was his nature, because he had been gripped tight by the pride of the trail and harness. It was the pride which holds dogs in the toil to the last grasp. They die joyfully in the harness, and their hearts break if they are cut out of the harness. This was the pride of Dave as wheel dog, of Sol-leks as he pulled with all his strength. It laid hold of them at break of camp, transforming them from sour and sullen brutes into straining, eager, ambitious creatures. It spurred them on all day. This was the pride that bore Spitz up and made him thrash the sled dogs who blundered and shirked or hid away at harness-up time in the morning. It was this pride that made Spitz fear Buck as a possible lead dog. And this was Buck's pride, too.

He openly threatened the other's leadership. He came between Spitz and the shirker he should have punished. And he did it deliberately. One night there was a heavy snowfall, and in the morning Pike, the shirker, did not appear. He was securely hidden in his nest under a foot of snow. Francois called him and sought him in vain. Spitz was wild with anger. He raged through the camp, smelling and digging in every likely place, snarling so frightfully that Pike heard and shivered in his hiding place.

But when he was at last unearthed, and Spitz flew at him to punish him, Buck flew, with equal rage, in between. So unexpected was it, and so shrewdly managed, that Spitz was hurled backward and off his feet. Pike, who had been trembling with fear, took heart at this and sprang upon his overthrown leader. Buck, to whom fair play was a forgotten code, likewise sprang upon Spitz. Francois, chuckling at the incident, but fair and just, brought his lash down upon Buck with all his might. This failed to drive Buck from his rival, and the butt of the whip was brought into play. Half stunned by the blow, Buck was knocked backward, and the lash laid upon him again and again, while Spitz soundly punished Pike.

In the days that followed, as Dawson grew closer and closer, Buck still continued to interfere between Spitz and the loafers. But he did it craftily, when Francois was not around. Following Buck's lead, the other dogs began to disobey the ruler. Dave and Sol-leks were loyal, but the rest of the team went from bad to worse. Things no longer went right. Trouble was always afoot, and at the bottom of it was Buck. He kept Francois busy, for the dog driver was in constant dread of the life-and-death struggle between the two which he knew must take place sooner or later. On more than one night the sounds of quarreling among the other dogs turned him out of his sleeping robe, fearful that Buck and Spitz were at it.

But the opportunity did not present itself, and they pulled into Dawson one dreary afternoon with the great fight still to come. Here were many men, and countless dogs, and Buck found them all at work. All day they swung up and down the main street in long teams, and in the night their jingling bells still went by. They hauled cabin logs and firewood, pulled freight up to the mines, and did all manner of work that horses did in the Santa Clara Valley. Here and there Buck met Southland dogs, but in the main they were the wild wolf Husky breed. Every night, regularly, at nine, at twelve, at three, they lifted a song, in which it was Buck's delight to join. Buck was strangely stirred by it. When he moaned and sobbed, it was with the pain of living that was the pain of his wild fathers, and the fear and mystery of the cold and dark that was to them fear and mystery.

Seven days from the time they pulled into Dawson, they dropped down the steep bank by the Barracks to the Yukon Trail, and pulled again for Dyea and Salt Water. Perrault was carrying back dispatches more important than those he had brought in. Also, the travel pride had gripped him, and he purposed to make the record trip of the year. Several things favored him in this. The week had rested the dogs and put them in trim. The trail they had broken into the country was packed hard. In two or three places the police had arranged food for dog and man, and they were traveling light.

They made Sixty Mile, which is a fifty-mile run, on the first day. The second day saw them booming up the Yukon River well on their way to Pelly. But such splendid running was achieved not without great trouble on the part of Francois. The revolt led by Buck had destroyed the loyal spirit of the team. It no longer was as one dog leaping in the harness. Buck led the others into all kinds of mischief. No more was Spitz a leader greatly to be feared. The old respect for him departed, and they grew equal to challenging his authority.

Pike robbed him of half a fish one night and gulped it down under the protection of Buck. Another night Dub and Joe fought Spitz and made him forego the punishment they deserved. And even Billee, the good-natured, was less good-natured. Buck never came near Spitz without snarling and bristling. In fact, his conduct approached that of a bully, and he was given to swaggering up and down before Spitz' very nose.

The breaking down of discipline likewise affected the dogs in their relations with one another. They quarreled more than ever among themselves, till at times the camp was filled with howling. Dave and Sol-leks alone behaved well. Francois stamped the snow in rage, and tore his hair. His lash was always singing among the dogs, but directly his back was

71

turned they were at it again. He backed up Spitz with his whip, while Buck backed up the remainder of the team.

Francois knew who was behind all the trouble, and Buck knew he knew. But Buck was too clever ever again to be caught red-handed. He worked faithfully in the harness, for the toil had become a delight to him. Yet it was a greater delight slyly to start a fight among his mates and tangle the harness straps.

At the mouth of the Tahkeena River, one night after supper, Dub saw a snowshoe rabbit, chased it, but missed. In a second the whole team was in full cry. A hundred yards away was a camp of the Northwest Police, with fifty dogs, Huskies all, who joined the chase. The rabbit sped down the river, turned off into a small creek and went up the frozen bed. It ran lightly on the surface of the snow, while the dogs plowed through by main strength.

Buck led the pack, sixty strong, around bend after bend, but he could not gain. He lay down low to the race, whining eagerly, his splendid body flashing forward, leap by leap, in the white moonlight. And leap by leap the snowshoe rabbit flashed on ahead. Buck, leading the pack, sounded the old wolf cry. He strained after the food that was alive and that fled swiftly before him through the moonlight.

Spitz left the pack and cut across a narrow neck of land where the creek made a long bend around. Buck did not know of this. And as he rounded the bend, he saw another and larger frost ghost leap from the overhanging bank into the immediate path of the rabbit. It was Spitz. The rabbit could not turn. As the white teeth broke its back in midair it shrieked as loudly as a stricken man may shriek. At sound of this, the full pack at Buck's heels raised a wild chorus of delight.

Buck did not cry out. He did not check himself, but drove in upon Spitz, shoulder to shoulder, so hard that he missed the throat. They rolled over and over in the powdery snow.

Spitz gained his feet slashing Buck down the shoulder and leaping clear. Twice his teeth clipped together like the steel jaws of a trap. He backed away for better footing, with lean and lifting lips that snarled.

In a flash Buck knew it. The time had come. It was to the death. They circled about, snarling, ears laid back, keenly watchful for the advantage. He seemed to remember it all— the white woods, and earth, and moonlight, and the thrill of battle. There was not the faintest whisper of air—nothing moved, not a leaf quivered. The visible breaths of the dogs rose slowly in the frosty air. They had made short work of the snowshoe rabbit, these dogs that were ill-tamed wolves. They were now drawn up in a waiting circle. They, too, were silent, their eyes only gleaming and their breaths drifting slowly upward. To Buck it seemed nothing new or strange, but a scene of old time. It was as though it had always been.

Spitz was a practiced fighter. From Spits-

bergen through the arctic, and across Canada and the Barrens, he had held his own with all manner of dogs. And he had won mastery over them. Bitter rage was his, but never blind rage. Ready to slash and destroy, he never forgot that his enemy was also ready to destroy. He never rushed till he was prepared to receive a rush, never attacked till he had first defended that attack.

In vain Buck strove to sink his teeth in the neck of the big white dog. Wherever his fangs struck for the softer flesh, they were countered by the fangs of Spitz. Fang clashed fang, and lips were cut and bleeding, but Buck could not get through his enemy's guard.

Buck took to rushing as though for the throat, but suddenly drawing back his head and curving in from the side. Then he would drive his shoulder at the shoulder of Spitz, as a ram by which to overthrow him. But instead, Buck's shoulder was slashed down each time as Spitz leaped lightly away.

76

Spitz was untouched, while Buck was streaming with blood and panting hard. The fight was growing desperate. And all the while the silent and wolfish circle waited to finish off the dog that went down. As Buck grew winded, Spitz took to rushing, and he kept him staggering for footing. Once Buck went over, and the whole circle of sixty dogs started up. But he recovered himself, almost in midair, and the circle sank down again and waited.

But Buck possessed a quality that made for greatness—imagination. He fought by instinct, but he could fight by head as well. He rushed, as though attempting the old shoulder trick, but at the last instant swept low to the snow and in. His teeth closed on Spitz' left foreleg. There was a crunch of breaking bone, and the white dog faced him on three legs. Three times Buck tried to knock him over, then repeated the trick and broke the right foreleg. Despite the pain and helplessness, Spitz struggled madly to keep up. He saw the silent circle, with gleaming eyes, lolling tongues, and silvery breaths drifting upward. They closed in upon him, and this time he was the one who was beaten.

There was no hope for him. Buck was without mercy. He went in for the final rush. The circle had tightened till he could feel the breaths of the Huskies on his flanks. He could see them, beyond Spitz and to either side, half crouching for the spring, their eyes fixed upon him. A pause seemed to fall. Every animal was motionless as though turned to stone. Only Spitz quivered and bristled as he staggered back and forth, snarling, as though to frighten off death.

Then Buck sprang in and out. But while he was in, shoulder had at last squarely met shoulder. The dark circle became a dot on the moonflooded snow as Spitz disappeared from view. Buck stood and looked on, the successful champion, the beast who had made his kill and found it good.

78

7

The Leader

"That Spitz fight like a devil," said Perrault, as he surveyed the gaping rips and cuts.

"And that Buck fight like two devils," was Francois' answer. "And now we make good time. No more Spitz, no more trouble, sure."

While Perrault packed the camp outfit and loaded the sled, the dog driver proceeded to harness the dogs. Buck trotted up to the place Spitz would have occupied as leader. But Francois, not noticing him, brought Sol-leks to the lead position. In Francois' judgment, Sol-leks was the best lead dog left. Buck sprang upon Sol-leks in a fury, driving him back and standing in his place.

"Eh? Eh?" Francois cried, slapping his thighs gleefully. "Look at that Buck. He kill that Spitz, then think to take the job."

"Go 'way, Chook!" he cried, but Buck refused to budge.

He took Buck by the neck, and though the dog growled threateningly, dragged him to one side and replaced Sol-leks. The old dog did not like it, and showed plainly that he was afraid of Buck. Francois was determined, but when he turned his back, Buck again displaced Sol-leks, who was not at all unwilling to go.

Francois was angry. "Now, I fix you!" he cried, coming back with a heavy club in his hand.

Buck remembered the man in the red sweater, and retreated slowly. Nor did he attempt to charge in when Sol-leks was once more brought forward. But he circled just beyond the range of the club, snarling with bitterness and rage. While he circled he watched the club so as to dodge it if thrown by Francois, for Buck had become wise in the way of clubs.

The driver went about his work. He called to Buck when he was ready to put him in his old place in front of Dave. Buck retreated two or three steps. Francois followed him up. Buck again retreated. After some time of this, Francois threw down the club, thinking that Buck feared a thrashing. But Buck was in open revolt. He wanted, not to escape a clubbing, but to have the leadership. It was his by right. He had earned it, and he would not be content with less.

Perrault took a hand. Between them they ran Buck about for the better part of an hour. They threw clubs at him. He dodged and snarled, and kept out of their reach. He did not try to run away, but retreated around and around the camp. He advertised plainly that when his desire was met, he would come in and be good.

Francois sat down and scratched his head. Perrault looked at his watch. Time was flying, and they should have been on the trail an hour gone. Francois scratched his head again. He shook it and grinned sheepishly at Perrault who shrugged his shoulders in a sign that they were beaten.

Then Francois went up to where Sol-leks stood and called to Buck. Buck laughed, as dogs laugh, yet kept his distance. Francois unfastened Sol-leks' harness straps and put him back in his old place. The team stood harnessed to the sled in an unbroken line, ready for the trail. There was no place for Buck save at the front. Once more Francois called, and once more Buck laughed and kept away.

"Throw down the club," Perrault commanded.

Francois obeyed. Then Buck trotted in, laughing triumphantly, and swung around into

position at the head of the team. His straps were fastened, and the sled broken out of the ice. With both men running, they dashed out on to the river trail.

Highly as the dog driver had valued Buck before, he found, while the day was yet young, that he had undervalued. At a bound Buck took up the duties of leadership. Where judgment was required, and quick thinking and quick acting, he showed himself superior even to Spitz, of whom Francois had never seen an equal.

But it was in giving the law and making his mates live up to it, that Buck excelled. Dave and Sol-leks did not mind the change in leadership. It was none of their business. Their business was to toil, and toil mightily, in the harness. So long as that was not interfered with, they did not care what happened. Billee, the good-natured, could lead for all they cared so long as he kept order. The rest of the team however, had grown unruly during the last days of Spitz. Their surprise was great now that Buck proceeded to lick them into shape.

Pike, who never put an ounce more of his weight against the breast band than he was compelled to do, was swiftly and repeatedly shaken for loafing. The first day he was pulling more than ever before in his life. The first night in camp, Joe, the sour one, was punished roundly—a thing that Spitz had never succeeded in doing. Buck simply smothered him by superior weight, and cut him up till he ceased snapping and began to whine for mercy.

The general tone of the team picked up immediately. Once more the dogs leaped as one dog in the harness. At the Rink Rapids two native Huskies, Teek and Koona, were added. The speed with which Buck broke them in took away Francois' breath.

"Never such a dog as that Buck! He's worth one thousand dollars. Eh, Perrault?"

And Perrault nodded. He was ahead of the record then, and gaining day by day. The trail was in excellent condition, well packed and hard, and there was no new-fallen snow with which to contend. It was not too cold. The temperature dropped to fifty below zero and remained there the whole trip. The men rode and ran by turn, and the dogs were kept on the jump with but infrequent stops.

The Thirty Mile River was well coated with ice. And they covered in one day going out what had taken them ten days coming in. In one run they made a sixty-mile dash from the foot of Lake Lebarge to the White Horse Rapids. Across Marsh, Tagish, and Bennett, seventy miles of lakes, they flew so fast that the man whose turn it was to run ahead, was towed behind the sled at the end of a rope.

On the last night of the second week, they topped White Pass. Soon they dropped down the sea slope with the lights of Skagway and of the ships at their feet.

It was a record run. Each day for fourteen days they had averaged forty miles. For three days Perrault and Francois pranced up and down the main street of Skagway and were deluged with invitations. The team was the constant center of a crowd of dog busters and drivers. This lasted until three or four western bad men tried to clean out the town, and were riddled like pepperboxes for their pains. Next came official orders. Francois called Buck to him, threw his arms around him, wept over him. And that was the last of Francois and Perrault. Like other men, they passed out of Buck's life for good.

Another half-breed took charge of him and his mates, and in company with a dozen other dog teams he started back over the weary trail to Dawson. It was no light running now, nor record time, but heavy toil each day, with a heavy load behind. For this was the mail train, carrying word from the world to the men who sought gold under the shadow of the North Pole.

Buck did not like it, but he stood up well

under the work, taking pride in it after the manner of Dave and Sol-leks. He saw that his mates, whether they prided in it or not, did their fair share. It was a dull life, operating with machine-like regularity. One day was very like another. At a certain time each morning the cooks turned out, fires were built, and breakfast was eaten. Then, while some broke camp, others harnessed the dogs, and they were under way an hour or so before dawn.

At night, camp was made. Some pitched the tents, others cut firewood and pine boughs for the beds. And still others carried water or ice for the cooks. Also, the dogs were fed. To them, this was the one feature of the day. It was good to loaf around, after the fish was eaten, for an hour or so with the five hundred other dogs. There were fierce fighters among them, but three battles with the fiercest made Buck the master. When he bristled and showed his teeth, they got out of his way.

8

Dave

It was a hard trip, with the mail behind them, and the heavy work wore them down. They were short of weight and in poor condition when they made Dawson, and should have had a ten days' or a week's rest at least. But in two days' time they dropped down the Yukon bank loaded with letters for the Outside. The dogs were tired, the drivers grumbling, and to make matters worse, it snowed every day. This meant a soft trail and heavier pulling for the dogs. Yet the drivers were fair through it all, and did their best for the animals.

Each night the dogs were attended to first. No man sought his sleeping robe till he had seen to the feet of the dogs he drove. Still, the dogs' strength went down. Since the beginning of the winter they had traveled eighteen hundred miles, dragging sleds the whole weary distance. And eighteen hundred miles will tell upon the life of the toughest. Buck stood it, keeping his mates up to their work and in order, though he, too, was very tired. Billee cried and whimpered regularly in his sleep each night. Joe was more sour than ever, and Sol-leks was unapproachable, blind side or other side.

But it was Dave who suffered most of all. Something had gone wrong with him. He became more moody and cross. When camp was pitched, he at once made his nest, where his driver fed him. Once out of the harness and down, he did not get on his feet again till harness-up time in the morning. Sometimes, when jerked by a sudden stop of the sled, or by straining to start it, he would cry out with pain.

The driver examined him, but could find nothing. All the drivers became interested in his case. They talked it over at mealtime, and over their last pipes before going to bed. One night they held a consultation. He was brought from his nest to the fire and they pressed and prodded him till he cried out many times. Something was wrong inside, but they could locate no broken bones, and could not make it out.

By the time Cassiar Bar was reached, he was so weak that he was falling repeatedly in harness. The half-breed called a halt and took him out of the team, making the next dog, Sol-leks, fast to the sled. His intention was to rest Dave, letting him run free behind the sled. Sick as he was, Dave resented being taken out.

When the sled started, he floundered in the

soft snow alongside the beaten trail. He attacked Sol-leks with his teeth, rushing against him and trying to thrust him off into the soft snow on the other side. He was striving to leap inside his harness straps and get between him and the sled. All the while he whined and yelped and cried with grief and pain.

The half-breed tried to drive him away with the whip, but Dave paid no heed to the stinging lash, and the man had not the heart to strike harder. Dave refused to run quietly on the trail behind the sled, where the going was easy. But he continued to flounder alongside in the soft snow, where the going was most difficult, till he was exhausted. Then he fell, and lay where he fell, howling as the long train of sleds churned by.

With the last remnant of his strength he managed to stagger along behind till the train made another stop. Then he floundered past the sleds to his own, where he stood beside Sol-leks. His driver lingered a moment to get a light for his pipe from the man behind. Then he returned and started his dogs. They swung out on the trail too easily, turned their heads, and stopped in surprise. The driver was surprised, too. The sled had not moved. He called his comrades to see the sight. Dave had bitten through both of Sol-leks' straps, and was standing directly in front of the sled in his proper place.

He pleaded with his eyes to remain there. The men talked of how a dog could break its heart through being denied the work that killed it. Also they held it a mercy, since Dave was to die anyway, that he should die in the harness, heart-easy and content. So he was harnessed in again, and proudly he pulled as of old, though more than once he cried out from the bite of his inward hurt. Several times he fell down and was dragged, and once the sled ran upon him so that he limped thereafter on one of his hind legs.

But he held out till camp was reached, when

his driver made a place for him by the fire. Morning found him too weak to travel. At harness-up time he tried to crawl to his driver. He got on his feet, staggered, and fell. Then he wormed his way forward slowly toward where the harnesses were being put on his mates. He would advance his forelegs and drag up his body with a sort of hitching movement. Then he would advance his forelegs and hitch ahead for a few more inches. His strength left him, and the last his mates saw of him he lay gasping in the snow and looking after them. But they could hear him mournfully howling till they passed out of sight behind a belt of river timber.

Here the train was halted. The half-breed slowly retraced his steps to the camp they had left. The men ceased talking. A revolver shot rang out. The man came back hurriedly. The whips snapped, the bells tinkled merrily, the sleds churned along the trail. Buck knew, and every dog knew what had taken place.

9

New Owners

Thirty days from the time the Salt Water Mail left Dawson, with Buck and his mates, it arrived at Skagway. They were in a wretched state, worn out and worn down. Buck's one hundred forty pounds had gone down to one hundred fifteen. His mates also had lost weight. Pike, the loafer, who, in his lifetime of deceit, had often successfully pretended a hurt leg, was now limping in earnest. Sol-leks was limping, and Dub was suffering from a wrenched shoulder blade.

They were all terribly footsore. No spring or rebound was left in them. Their feet fell heavily on the trail, jarring their bodies and doubling the fatigue of a day's travel. There was nothing the matter with them except that they were dead tired.

It was not the dead tiredness that comes through brief and extreme effort, from which recovery is a matter of hours. It was the dead tiredness that comes through months of toil. There was no power of recovery left, no reserve strength to call upon. It had all been used, the last least bit of it. Every muscle, every cell, was tired, dead tired. And there was reason for it. In less than five months they had traveled twenty-five hundred miles. And during the last eighteen hundred miles they had had but five days' rest. When they arrived at Skagway they were apparently on their last legs. They could barely keep the harness straps tight, and on the downgrades just managed to keep out of the way of the sled.

"Mush on, poor sore feet," the driver encouraged them as they tottered down the main street of Skagway. "This is the last. Then we get one long rest. Eh? For sure. One big long rest."

The drivers confidently expected a long stopover. They themselves had covered twelve hundred miles with two days' rest. In the nature of reason and common justice they deserved a little time for loafing. So many men had rushed into the Klondike. And so many sweethearts and wives had not rushed in, that the mail was piled high. Also, there were official orders. Fresh batches of Hudson Bay dogs were to take the places of those worthless for the trail. The worthless ones were to be got rid of, and since dogs count for little against dollars, they were to be sold.

Three days passed, by which time Buck and his mates found how really tired and weak they were. Then, on the morning of the fourth day, two men from the States came along and bought them, harness and all, for a song.

The men addressed each other as "Hal" and "Charles." Charles was a middle-aged, fair-haired man, with weak and watery eyes and a mustache that twisted fiercely up. It concealed a limply drooping lip. Hal was a youngster of nineteen or twenty, with a big Colt revolver and a hunting knife strapped about him on a belt that fairly bristled with bullets.

Buck heard the bargaining and saw the money pass between Charles and the government agent. He knew that the half-breed and the mail-train drivers were passing out of his life as Perrault and Francois and the others had gone before. When driven with his mates to the new owners' camp, Buck saw a slipshod affair, tent half stretched, dishes unwashed, everything in disorder. Also, he saw a woman. "Mercedes" the men called her. She was Charles' wife and Hal's sister—a nice family party.

Buck watched them uneasily as they proceeded to take down the tent and load the sled. There was a great deal of effort about their manner, but no businesslike order. The tent was rolled into an awkward bundle three times as large as it should have been. The tin dishes were packed away unwashed. Mercedes continually fluttered in the way of her men and kept up an unbroken chattering of protest and advice. When they put a clothes sack on the front of the sled, she suggested it should go on the back. And so they put it on the back, and covered it over with a couple of other bundles. Then she discovered overlooked articles which could go nowhere else but in that very sack, and the men unloaded again.

Three men from a neighboring tent came out and looked on, grinning and winking at one another.

"You've got a right smart load as it is," said one of them. "It's not me should tell you your business, but I wouldn't take that tent along if I were you."

"Undreamed of!" cried Mercedes, throwing up her hands. "How in the world could I manage without a tent?"

"It's springtime, and you won't get any more cold weather," the man replied.

She shook her head decidedly, and Charles and Hal put the last odds and ends on top of the mountainous load.

"Think it'll ride?" one of the men asked.

"Why shouldn't it?" Charles demanded rather shortly.

"Oh, that's all right, that's all right," the man hastened to say. "I was just wondering, that is all. It seemed a little top heavy."

Charles turned his back and drew the ropes down as well as he could, which was not in the least well.

"And of course the dogs can hike along all day with that contraption behind them," said a second man.

"Certainly," said Hal, with freezing politeness, taking hold of the gee pole with one

100

hand and swinging his whip from the other. "Mush!" he shouted. "Mush on there!"

The dogs sprang against the breast bands, strained hard for a few moments, then relaxed. They were unable to move the sled.

"The lazy brutes! I'll show them," he cried, preparing to lash out at them with the whip.

But Mercedes interfered, crying, "Oh, Hal, you mustn't," as she caught hold of the whip and wrenched it from him. "The poor dears! Now you must promise you won't be harsh with them for the rest of the trip, or I won't go a step."

"Precious lot you know about dogs," her brother sneered. "I wish you'd leave me alone. They're lazy, I tell you, and you've got to whip them to get anything out of them. That's their way. You ask anyone. Ask one of those men."

Mercedes looked at them, pain written in her pretty face.

"They're weak as water, if you want to

know," came the reply from one of the men. "Completely tuckered out, that's what's the matter. They need a rest."

"Rest be blanked," said Hal, with his beardless lips. Mercedes said, "Oh!" in pain and sorrow.

But she rushed at once to the defense of her brother. "Never mind that man," she said. "You're driving our dogs, and you do what you think best with them."

Again Hal's whip fell upon the dogs. They threw themselves against the breast bands, dug their feet into the packed snow. They got down low to it, and put forth all their strength. The sled held as though it were an anchor. After two efforts, they stood still, panting. The whip whistled savagely, when once more Mercedes interfered. She dropped on her knees before Buck, with tears in her eyes, and put her arms around his neck.

"You poor, poor dears," she cried, "why don't you pull hard? Then you won't be whipped." Buck did not like her, but he was feeling too miserable to avoid her, taking it as part of the day's miserable work.

One of the onlookers, who had been clenching his teeth, now spoke up, "It's not that I care a whoop what becomes of you, but for the dogs' sakes I just want to tell you. You can help them a mighty lot by breaking out that sled. The runners are frozen fast. Throw your weight against the gee pole, right and left, and break it out."

A third time the attempt was made, but this time, following the advice, Hal broke out the runners which had been frozen to the snow. The overloaded and top-heavy sled forged ahead, Buck and his mates struggling frantically under the rain of blows.

A hundred yards ahead, the path turned and sloped steeply into the main street. It would have required an experienced man to keep the top-heavy sled upright, and Hal was not such a man. As they swung on the turn the

103

sled went over, spilling half its load through the loose ropes. The dogs never stopped. The lightened sled bounded on its side behind them. They were angry because of the beatings they had received and the unjust load. Buck was raging. He broke into a run, the team following his lead. Hal cried "Whoa! whoa!" but they gave no heed. He tripped and was pulled off his feet. The dogs dashed on and added to the gaiety of Skagway as they scattered the remainder of the outfit along its main street.

Kind-hearted citizens caught the dogs and gathered up the scattered belongings. Also, they gave advice. "Half the load and twice the dogs, if you ever expect to reach Dawson," was what they said.

Hal and his sister and brother-in-law listened unwillingly, pitched tent, and began to repack the outfit. Canned goods were turned out that made men laugh, for canned goods on the Long Trail was a thing to dream about.

"Blankets for a hotel," said one of the men who laughed and helped. "Half as many is too much. Get rid of them. Throw away that tent, and all those dishes. Who's going to wash them, anyway? Do you think you're traveling on a Pullman?"

And so it went. Mercedes cried when her clothes bags were dumped on the ground and article after article was thrown out. She cried in general, and she cried in particular over each discarded thing. She said she would not go an inch. She appealed to everybody and to everything, finally wiping her eyes and proceeding to cast out even articles that were necessary. And when she had finished with her own, she attacked the belongings of her men and went through them like a whirlwind.

This accomplished, the outfit, though cut in half, was still too much for the dogs to pull. Charles and Hal went out in the evening and bought six Outside dogs. These, added to the six of the original team, and Teek and Koona, the Huskies obtained at the Rink Rapids on the record trip, brought the team up to fourteen. But the Outside dogs, though practically broken in since their landing, did not amount to much. Three were short-haired pointers, one was a Newfoundland, and the other two were of a mixed breed. These newcomers did not seem to know anything. Buck and his comrades looked upon them with disgust, and though he speedily taught them their places and what not to do, he could not teach them what to do.

They did not take kindly to harness and trail. They were bewildered and spirit broken by the strange savage environment and by the ill treatment they had received. The two mixed breeds were without spirit at all. Bones were the only things breakable about them.

With the newcomers hopeless and forlorn, and the old team worn out by twenty-five hundred miles of travel, the outlook was anything but bright. The two men, however, were quite cheerful. And they were proud, too. They were doing the thing in style, with fourteen dogs. They had seen other sleds depart over the White Pass for Dawson or come in from Dawson. But never had they seen a sled with so many as fourteen dogs.

In the nature of arctic travel there was a reason why fourteen dogs should not drag one sled, and that was that one sled could not carry the food for fourteen dogs. But Charles and Hal did not know this. They had worked the trip out with a pencil, so much to a dog, so many dogs, so many days. Mercedes looked over their shoulders and nodded. It was all so very simple.

10

Starvation

Late next morning Buck led the long team up the street. There was nothing lively about it, no snap or go in him and his fellows. They were starting dead weary. Four times he had covered the distance between Salt Water and Dawson. The knowledge that, worn out and tired, he was facing the same trail once more, made him bitter. His heart was not in the work, nor was the heart of any dog. The Outside dogs were timid and frightened, the Inside dogs without confidence in their masters.

Buck felt vaguely that there was no depending upon these two men and the woman. They did not know how to do anything, and as the days went by it became apparent that they could not learn. They were slack in all things and without order. It took them half the night to pitch a careless camp, and half the morning to break camp and get the sled loaded. The rest of the day they were occupied in stopping and rearranging the load. Some days they did not make ten miles. On other days they were unable to get started at all. And on no day did they succeed in making more than half the distance used by the men as a basis in figuring how much dog food they would need.

It was natural that they should go short on dog food. But they hastened it by overfeeding, bringing the day nearer when underfeeding would begin. The Outside dogs, whose digestions had not been trained by starvation to make the most of little, had huge appetites. And when, in addition to this, the worn-out

Huskies pulled weakly, Hal decided that the ration was too small. He doubled it. And to cap it all, when Mercedes, with tears in her pretty eyes, could not coax him into giving the dogs still more, she stole from the fish sacks and fed them slyly. But it was not food that Buck and the Huskies needed. It was rest. And though they were making poor time, the heavy load they dragged sapped their strength severely.

Then came the underfeeding. Hal awoke one day to the fact that his dog food was half gone and the distance only quarter covered. And also for love or money no additional dog food was to be obtained. So he cut down even the regular ration and tried to increase the day's travel.

It was a simple matter to give the dogs less food, but it was impossible to make the dogs travel faster. Their own inability to get under way earlier in the morning prevented them from traveling longer hours. Not only did they not know how to work dogs, but they did not know how to work themselves.

The first to go was Dub. Poor blundering thief that he was, always getting caught and punished, he had none the less been a faithful worker. His wrenched shoulder blade, untreated and unrested, went from bad to worse, till finally Hal shot him with the big Colt revolver.

It is a saying of the country that an Outside dog starves to death on the ration of the Husky. So the six Outside dogs under Buck could do no less than die on half the ration of the Husky. The Newfoundland went first, followed by the three short-haired pointers, the two mixed breeds hanging longer on to life, but going, too, in the end.

By this time all the gentleness of the Southland had fallen away from the three people. Arctic travel became to them a reality too harsh for their manhood and womanhood. Mercedes ceased weeping over the dogs, being too occupied with weeping over herself and with quarreling with her husband and brother. To quarrel was the one thing they were never too weary to do. Their quarrels rose out of their misery and increased with it. The wonderful patience of the trail sometimes comes to men who toil hard and suffer, but remain sweet of speech and kindly. It did not come to these two men and the woman. They had no idea of such patience. They were stiff and in pain. Their muscles ached, their bones ached, their very hearts ached. Because of this they became sharp of speech, and hard words were first on their lips in the morning and last at night.

Charles and Hal argued whenever Mercedes gave them a chance. It was the belief of each that he did more than his share of the work. Neither hesitated to speak this belief at every opportunity. Sometimes Mercedes sided with her husband, sometimes with her brother. The result was a beautiful and unending family quarrel. In the meantime the fire remained unbuilt, the camp half pitched, and the dogs unfed.

Mercedes was pretty and soft, and had been treated well all her days. But the present treatment by her husband and brother was not even polite. It was her custom to be helpless. They complained, and she made their lives unendurable. She no longer considered the dogs, and because she was sore and tired, she insisted in riding on the sled. She was pretty and soft, but she weighed one hundred twenty pounds —a last straw to the load dragged by the weak and starving animals. She rode for days, till they fell in the harness and the sled stood still. Charles and Hal begged her to get off and walk, pleaded with her while she wept.

On one occasion they took her off the sled by main strength. They never did it again. She let her legs go limp like a spoiled child, and sat down on the trail. They went on their way but she did not move. After they had traveled three miles they unloaded the sled, came back for her, and by main strength put her on the sled again.

In their own misery they disregarded the suffering of their animals. Hal's theory, which he practiced on others, was that one must get hardened. He had started out preaching it to his sister and brother-in-law. Failing there, he hammered it into the dogs with a club.

At the Five Fingers the dog food gave out, and a toothless old squaw offered to trade them a few pounds of frozen horse hide for the Colt revolver that kept the big hunting knife company at Hal's hip. A poor substitute for food was this hide, just as it had been stripped from the starved horses of the cattle-men six months back. In its frozen state it was more like strips of iron. When a dog wrestled it into his stomach it thawed into thin leathery strings and into a mass of short hair, irritating and indigestible.

And through it all Buck staggered along at

115

the head of the team as in a nightmare. He pulled when he could. When he could no longer pull, he fell down and remained down till blows from whip or club drove him to his feet again. All the stiffness and gloss had gone out of his beautiful furry coat. The hair hung down, limp and draggled, or matted with dried blood where Hal's club had bruised him. His muscles had wasted away to knotty strings, and the flesh pads had disappeared. Each rib and every bone in his frame were outlined cleanly through the loose hide that was wrinkled in folds of emptiness. It was heartbreaking, but Buck's heart was unbreakable. The man in the red sweater had proved that.

As it was with Buck, so was it with his mates. They were just walking skeletons. There were seven altogether, including him. In their very great misery they hardly felt the bite of the lash or the bruise of the club now. The pain of the beating was dull and distant, just as the things their eyes saw and their ears heard seemed dull and distant. They were not half living, or quarter living. They were simply so many bags of bones in which sparks of life fluttered faintly. When a halt was made, they dropped down in the harness like dead dogs. The spark dimmed and paled and seemed to go out. When the club or whip fell upon them, the spark fluttered feebly up, and they tottered to their feet and staggered on.

There came a day when Billee, the good-natured, fell and could not rise. Hal had traded off his revolver so he took the ax and knocked Billee on the head as he lay in the harness, then cut the carcass out of the harness and dragged it to one side. Buck saw, and his mates saw, and they knew that this thing was very close to them. On the next day Koona went, and but five of them remained. Joe was too far gone to be mean. Pike, crippled and limping was only half conscious and not conscious enough any longer to loaf. Solleks, the one-eyed, was still faithful to the toil of harness and trail, and mournful in that he had so little strength with which to pull. Teek, who had not traveled so far that winter, was now beaten more than the others because he was fresher. And Buck, still at the head of the team, was no longer enforcing order or trying to enforce it. He was blind with weakness half the time and keeping the trail by the loom of it and by the dim feel of his feet.

11

Rescued

It was beautiful spring weather, but neither dogs nor humans were aware of it. Each day the sun rose earlier and set later. It was dawn by three in the morning, and twilight lingered till nine at night. The whole long day was a blaze of sunshine. The ghostly winter silence had given way to the great spring murmur of awakening life.

This murmur arose from all the land, filled

with the joy of living. It came from the things that lived and moved again, things which had been as dead and which had not moved during the long months of frost. The sap was rising in the pines. The willow and aspen trees were bursting out in young buds. Shrubs and vines were putting on fresh green. Crickets sang in the nights, and in the days all manner of creeping, crawling things rustled forth into the sun. Partridges and woodpeckers were booming and knocking in the forest. Squirrels were chattering, birds singing, and overhead honked the wild fowl driving up from the south in cunning wedges that split the air.

From every hill slope came the trickle of running water, the music of unseen fountains. All things were thawing, bending, snapping. The Yukon River was straining to break loose the ice that bound it down. The water ate away from beneath, while the sun ate from above. Air holes formed, cracks sprang and spread apart, while thin sections of ice fell

120

through bodily into the river. And amid all this bursting and throbbing of awakening life, under the blazing sun and through the soft-sighing breezes, staggered the two men, the woman, and the five Huskies. With the dogs falling, and Mercedes weeping and riding, they staggered into John Thornton's camp at the mouth of the White River. When they halted, the dogs dropped down as though they had all been struck dead.

Mercedes dried her eyes and looked at John Thornton. Charles sat down stiffly on a log rest. Hal did the talking. John Thornton was whittling the last touches on an ax handle he had made from a stick of birch. He whittled and listened, gave short replies, and, when it was asked, brief advice. He knew the breed, and he gave his advice certain that it would not be followed.

"They told us up above that the bottom was dropping out of the trail. And the best thing for us to do was to lie over," Hal said.

Thornton warned them to take no more chances on the melting ice.

"They told us we couldn't make White River, and here we are."

"And they told you true," John Thornton answered. "The bottom's likely to drop out at any moment. Only fools, with the blind luck of fools, could have made it. I tell you straight, I wouldn't risk my life on that ice for all the gold in Alaska."

"That's because you're not a fool, I suppose," said Hal. "All the same, we'll go on to Dawson." He uncoiled his whip. "Get up there, Buck! Hi! Get up there! Mush on!"

Thornton went on whittling. It was idle, he knew, to get between a fool and his folly.

But the team did not get up at the command. It had long since passed into the stage where blows were required to rouse it. The whip flashed out here and there. John Thornton bit his lips.

Sol-leks was the first to crawl to his feet.

Teek followed. Joe came next, yelping with pain. Pike made painful efforts. Twice he fell over when half up, and on the third attempt managed to rise. Buck made no effort. He lay quietly where he had fallen. The lash bit into him again and again, but he neither whined nor struggled.

Several times Thornton started to speak, but changed his mind. A moisture came into his eyes, and, as the whipping continued, he arose and walked up and down.

This was the first time Buck had failed, in itself a sufficient reason to drive Hal into a rage. He exchanged the whip for the club. Buck refused to move under the rain of heavier blows which now fell upon him. Like his mates, he was barely able to get up, but, unlike them, he had made up his mind not to get up. He had a vague feeling of death. This had been strong upon him when he pulled in to the bank, and it had not departed from him. With the thin and melting ice he had felt under his feet all day, he sensed disaster close at hand. It was out there ahead on the ice where his master was trying to drive him.

He refused to stir. So greatly had he suffered, and so far gone was he, that the blows did not hurt much. And as they continued to fall upon him, the spark of life within flickered and went down. It was nearly out. He felt strangely numb. As though from a great distance, he was aware that he was being beaten. But all pain had left him. He no longer felt anything, though very faintly he could hear the stroke of the club upon his body. But it was no longer his body, it seemed so far away.

And then, suddenly, without warning, uttering a cry John Thornton sprang upon the man who wielded the club. Hal was hurled backward, as though struck by a falling tree. Mercedes screamed. Charles looked on, wiped his watery eyes, but did not get up because of his stiffness.

124

John Thornton stood over Buck, struggling to control himself, too shaken with rage to speak.

"If you strike that dog again, I'll kill you," he at last managed to say in a choking voice.

"It's my dog," Hal replied, wiping the blood from his mouth as he came back. "Get out of my way, or I'll fix you. I'm going to Dawson."

Thornton stood between him and Buck, with no thought of getting out of the way. Hal drew his long hunting knife. Mercedes screamed. Thornton rapped Hal's knuckles with the ax handle, knocking the knife to the ground. He rapped his knuckles again as he tried to pick it up. Then he stooped, picked it up himself, and with two strokes cut Buck's harness.

Hal had no fight left in him. His hands were full with his sister, or his arms, rather. Besides Buck was too near dead to be of further use in hauling the sled.

A few minutes later they pulled out from the bank and down the river. Buck heard them go and raised his head to see. Pike was leading, Sol-leks was at the wheel position, and between were Joe and Teek. They were limping and staggering. Mercedes was riding the loaded sled. Hal guided at the gee pole, and Charles stumbled along in the rear.

As Buck watched them, Thornton knelt beside him and with rough kindly hands searched for broken bones. By the time his search had disclosed nothing more than many bruises and a state of terrible starvation, the sled was a quarter mile away. Dog and man watched it crawling along over the river ice.

Suddenly, they saw its back end drop down, as into a rut, and the gee pole, with Hal clinging to it, jerk into the air. Mercedes' scream came to their ears. They saw Charles turn and make one step to run back, and then a whole section of ice gave way and dogs and humans disappeared. A yawning hole was all that was

to be seen. The bottom had dropped out of the river trail.

John Thornton and Buck looked at each other.

"You poor devil," said John Thornton, and Buck licked his hand.

12

Loved

John Thornton had frozen his feet in December. His partners had made him comfortable and left him to get well, while they went up the river to get out a raft of sawed logs for Dawson. Thornton was still limping when he rescued Buck, but with the continued warm weather even the slight limp left him. Buck lay by the riverbank through the long spring days, and watched the running water. He listened lazily to the songs of birds and slowly won back his strength.

129

A rest comes very good after one has traveled three thousand miles. Buck became lazy as his wounds healed, his muscles swelled out, and the flesh finally came back to cover his bones.

For that matter, all were loafing—Buck, John Thornton, and Skeet and Nig. They were waiting for the raft to come that was to carry them down to Dawson.

Skeet was a little Irish setter, who early made friends with Buck. In his dying condition, Buck was unable to resent her first advances. She had the doctor instinct which some dogs possess. As a mother cat washes her kittens, so she washed and cleaned Buck's wounds. Each morning after he had finished his breakfast, she performed her self-appointed task, till he came to look for her as much as he did for Thornton. Nig, equally friendly, was a huge, black, good-natured dog, half bloodhound and half deerhound with eyes that laughed.

To Buck's surprise these dogs showed no jealousy toward him. They seemed to share the kindliness of John Thornton. As Buck grew stronger they drew him into all sorts of ridiculous games, in which Thornton himself joined. In this fashion Buck romped into a new life. Love, genuine love, was his for the first time. This he had never experienced at Judge Miller's down in the sun-kissed Santa Clara Valley. With the Judge's sons, hunting and tramping, his had been a working partnership. With the Judge's grandsons it was a sort of guardianship, and with the Judge himself, a stately and dignified friendship. But it had taken John Thornton to arouse love that was feverish and burning.

This man had saved his life, which was something, but, further, he was the ideal master. Other men saw to the welfare of their dogs from a sense of duty and business. He saw to the welfare of his dogs as if they were his own children, because he could not help it. And he saw further. He never forgot a kindly greeting or a cheering word. To sit down for a long talk with them ("gas" he called it) was as much his delight as theirs. He had a way of taking Buck's head roughly between his hands, and resting his own head upon Buck's. He would shake Buck back and forth, calling him names that to Buck were love names.

Buck knew no greater joy than that rough embrace. And when released he sprang to his feet, his mouth laughing. John Thornton would exclaim, "You can all but speak!"

Buck had a trick of love expression that was akin to hurt. He would often seize Thornton's hand in his mouth and close so fiercely that the flesh bore the marks of his teeth. But the man understood this bite for a caress.

While Buck went wild with happiness when Thornton touched him or spoke to him, he did not seek attention. Skeet would shove her nose under Thornton's hand and nudge and

nudge till petted. Nig would stalk up and rest his great head on Thornton's knee. But Buck was content to adore at a distance. He would lie by the hour, eager, alert, at Thornton's feet, looking up into his face, dwelling upon it, studying it, following with keenest interest each fleeting expression, every movement or change of feature. Or, as chance might have it, he would lie farther away, to the side or rear, watching the outlines of the man and the occasional movements of his body. And often the strength of Buck's gaze would draw John Thornton's head around, and he would return the gaze, without speech. His heart would shine out of his eyes as Buck's heart shone out.

For a long time after his rescue, Buck did not like Thornton to get out of his sight. From the moment he left the tent to when he entered it again, Buck would follow at his heels. His masters since he had come into the Northland had bred in him a fear that no master could

134

endure. He was afraid that Thornton would pass out of his life as Perrault and Francois and the half-breed had passed out. Even in the night, in his dreams, he was haunted by this fear. At such times he would shake off sleep and creep through the chill to the flap of the tent. He would stand and listen to the sound of his master's breathing.

But in spite of this great love he bore John Thornton, the strain of the wildness which the Northland had aroused in him, remained alive and active. Buck was faithful and devoted yet he retained his wildness. He was a thing of the wild, come in from the wild to sit by John Thornton's fire. He was not a dog of the soft Southland stamped with the marks of civilization. Because of his very great love, he could not steal from this man.

His face and body were scored by the teeth of many dogs, and he fought as fiercely as ever and more shrewdly. Skeet and Nig were too good-natured for quarreling—besides, they belonged to John Thornton. But a strange dog swiftly acknowledged Buck's supremacy or found himself struggling for life. And Buck was merciless. He had learned well the law of club and fang. He never lost an advantage or drew back from a foe he had started on the way to death.

He had learned from Spitz, and from the chief fighting dogs of the Northwest Police and mail, and knew there was no middle course. He must master or be mastered. To show mercy was a weakness. Mercy did not exist in the wild life. It was misunderstood for fear, and such misunderstandings made for death. Kill or be killed, eat or be eaten, was the law, and this law, he obeyed.

He sat by John Thornton's fire, a broad-breasted dog, white-fanged and long-furred. But through him he seemed to feel a memory of all manner of dogs, half-wolves and wild wolves.

Each day mankind and the claims of mankind slipped further from him. Deep in the forest a call was sounding. As often as he heard this call, he felt compelled to plunge into the forest, and on and on, he knew not where or why. Nor did he wonder where or why the call was sounding deep in the forest. As often as he gained the soft unbroken earth and the green shade, the love for John Thornton drew him back again.

Thornton alone held him. The rest of mankind was as nothing. Travelers might praise or pet him, but he was cold under it all. From some men he would get up and walk away. When Thornton's partners, Hans and Pete, arrived on the long-expected raft, Buck refused to notice them till he learned they were close to Thornton. They were of the same large type as Thornton, living close to the earth, thinking simply and seeing clearly. Before they swung the raft into the big eddy by the saw mill at Dawson, they understood Buck and his ways.

For Thornton, however, his love seemed to grow and grow. He, alone among men, could put a pack upon Buck's back in the summer traveling. Nothing was too great for Buck to do, when Thornton commanded. The men grubstaked themselves from the proceeds of the raft and left Dawson for the head waters of the Tanana River. One day the men and dogs were sitting on the crest of a cliff which fell three hundred feet to bare bed rock below. John Thornton was sitting near the edge, Buck at his shoulder. A thoughtless whim seized Thornton, and he drew the attention of Hans and Pete to the experiment he had in mind.

"Jump, Buck!" he commanded sweeping his arm out and over the chasm. The next instant he was grappling with Buck on the extreme edge, while Hans and Pete were dragging them back into safety.

"It's uncanny," Pete said after it was over and they could speak.

Thornton shook his head. "No, it is splendid, and it is terrible, too. Do you know, it sometimes makes me afraid."

"I'll not be the man that lays hands on you while he's around," Pete announced, nodding his head toward Buck.

"By jingo!" was Hans' contribution. "Me neither."

It was at Circle City that Pete's fears were realized. "Blackie" Burton had been picking a quarrel with a tenderfoot when Thornton stepped good-naturedly between. Buck, as was his custom, was lying in a corner, head on paws, watching his master's every action. Burton struck out, without warning, straight from the shoulder. Thornton was sent spinning, and just saved himself from falling.

Those who were looking on heard what was neither bark nor yelp, but something which is best described as a roar. They saw Buck's body rise up in the air as he left the floor for Burton's throat. The man saved his life by throwing out his arm, but was hurled backward to the floor with Buck on top of him. Buck loosed his teeth from the flesh of the arm and drove in again for the throat. This time the man succeeded in only partly blocking, and his throat was torn open. Then the crowd was upon Buck, and he was driven off. While a surgeon checked the bleeding, Buck prowled up and down, growling furiously, attempting to rush in, and being forced back by clubs. A meeting, called on the spot, decided that the dog had sufficient cause for his attack and Buck was discharged. But his reputation was made, and from that day his name spread through every camp in Alaska.

13

$1000

Later on, in the fall of the year, Buck saved John Thornton's life in quite another fashion. The three partners were in a long and narrow poling boat on a bad stretch of rapids on the Forty Mile Creek. Hans and Pete got out and moved along the bank, holding the boat rope. Thornton remained in the boat, helping its descent by means of a pole, and shouting directions to the shore. Buck, on the bank, worried and anxious, kept abreast of the boat, his eyes never off his master.

At a particularly bad spot, where a ledge of rocks jutted out into the river, Hans cast off the rope. While Thornton poled the boat out into the stream, Hans ran down the bank with the end in his hand to snub the boat when it had cleared that ledge. This it did, and was flying downstream in a current as swift as a mill race, when Hans checked it with the rope and checked too suddenly. The boat upset and snubbed in to the bank bottom up, while Thornton was flung out of it. He was carried downstream toward the worst part of the rapids, a stretch of wild water in which no one could swim.

Buck had sprung in on the instant, and at the end of three hundred yards, amid a mad swirl of water, overtook Thornton. When he felt Thornton grasp his tail, Buck headed for the bank, swimming with all his splendid strength. But the progress shoreward was slow. The progress downstream was amazingly rapid. From below came the fatal roaring where the wild current went wilder, and the rocks thrust through the water like the teeth of an enormous comb. The water was frightful, and Thornton knew that the shore was impossible. He scraped furiously over a rock, bruised across a second, and struck a third with crushing force. He released Buck and clutched the slippery rock with both hands. Above the roar of the churning water he shouted, "Go, Buck! Go!"

Buck could not hold his own, and swept on downstream, struggling desperately, but unable to win back. When he heard Thornton's command repeated, he partly reared out of the water, throwing his head high. Then he turned obediently toward the bank. He swam powerfully and was dragged ashore by Pete and Hans at the very point where swimming ceased to be possible.

They knew that the time a man could cling

to a slippery rock in that driving current was a matter of minutes. They ran as fast as they could up the bank to a point far above where Thornton was hanging on. They attached the rope to Buck's neck and shoulders. They were careful that it should neither strangle him nor slow his swimming, and launched him into the stream. He struck out boldly, but not straight enough into the stream. He discovered the mistake too late. Thornton was abreast of him and only a half-dozen strokes away, while he was being carried helplessly past.

Hans promptly snubbed with the rope, as though Buck were a boat. The rope tightened on him in the sweep of the current. He was jerked under. And under the water he remained till his body struck against the bank and he was hauled out. He was half drowned, and Hans and Pete threw themselves upon him, pounding the breath into him and the water out of him. He staggered to his feet and fell down.

The faint sound of Thornton's voice came to them, and though they could not make out the words of it, they knew that he was in trouble. His master's voice acted on Buck like an electric shock. He sprang to his feet and ran up the bank ahead of the men to the point of his previous departure.

Again the rope was attached and he was launched, and again struck out, but this time straight into the stream. He had misjudged once, but he would not be guilty of it a second time. Hans let out the rope, permitting no slack, while Pete kept it clear of coils. Buck held on till he was on a line straight above Thornton. Then he turned, and with the speed of an express train headed down upon him. Thornton saw him coming and Buck struck him like a battering ram. With the whole force of the current behind him, he reached up and closed with both arms around the shaggy neck. Hans snubbed the rope around the tree, and Buck and Thornton were jerked under the water. Choking, gasping for air, dragging over the jagged bottom, smashing against rocks and snags, they came in to the bank.

Thornton came to, face downward and being violently rolled back and forth across a drift log by Hans and Pete. His first glance was for Buck, over whose limp and apparently lifeless body Nig was setting up a howl, while Skeet was licking the wet face and closed eyes. Thornton was bruised and battered. He went carefully over Buck's body and found three broken ribs.

"That settles it," he announced. "We camp right here." And camp they did, till Buck's ribs knitted and he was able to travel.

That winter, at Dawson, Buck performed another exploit that put his name many notches higher on the totem pole of Alaskan fame. This exploit was particularly fortunate to the three men. They stood in need of the outfit which it furnished, and were enabled to make a long-desired trip into the east, where miners had not yet appeared.

It was brought about by a conversation in which men were boasting of their favorite dogs. Buck because of his record, was the target for these men, and Thornton was driven to defend him. At the end of half an hour one man stated that his dog could start a sled with five hundred pounds and walk off with it. A second bragged six hundred pounds for his dog, and a third, seven hundred.

"Pooh! Pooh!" said John Thornton. "Buck can start a thousand pounds."

"And break it out of the ice? And walk off with it for a hundred yards?" demanded Matthewson, who had made the seven hundred boast.

"And break it out, and walk off with it for a hundred yards," John Thornton said coolly.

"Well," Matthewson said slowly, so that all could hear, "I've got a thousand dollars that says he can't. And there it is." So saying, he slammed a big sack of gold dust down upon the table.

Nobody spoke. Thornton's bluff, if bluff it was, had been called. He could feel a flush of warm blood creeping up his face. His tongue had tricked him. He did not know whether Buck could start a thousand pounds. Half a ton! He had great faith in Buck's strength and had often thought him capable of starting such a load. But never, as now had he faced the possibility of it. The eyes of a dozen men were fixed upon him, silent and waiting. Besides, he had no thousand dollars. Neither had Hans or Pete.

"I've got a sled standing outside now, with twenty fifty-pound sacks of flour on it," Matthewson went on. "So don't let that hinder you."

Thornton did not reply. He did not know what to say. He glanced from face to face in the absent way of a man who has lost the power of thought and is seeking somewhere to find the thing that will start it going again. The face of Jim O'Brien, an old-time comrade, caught his eyes. And John Thornton did what he would never have dreamed of doing.

"Can you lend me a thousand?" he asked, almost in a whisper.

"Sure," answered O'Brien, thumping a big sack by the side of Matthewson's. "Though it's little faith I'm having, John, that the beast can do the trick."

The room emptied its occupants into the street to see the test. Several hundred men, furred and mittened, banked around the sled within easy distance. Matthewson's sled, loaded with a thousand pounds of flour, had been standing for a couple of hours. In the extreme cold, sixty below zero, the runners had frozen fast to the hard-packed snow. Men offered bets of two to one that Buck could not budge the sled.

An argument arose concerning the phrase "break out." O'Brien said that Thornton had the right to knock the runners loose, leaving Buck to "break it out" from a dead stand-still. Matthewson insisted that the phrase included breaking the runners from the frozen grip of the snow. A majority of the men who had witnessed the making of the bet decided in his favor. The odds went up to three to one against Buck.

There were no takers. Not a man believed Buck capable. Thornton had been hurried into the bet and was full of doubt. Now that he looked at the sled itself, with the regular team of ten dogs curled up in the snow before it, the more impossible the task appeared.

"Three to one!" Matthewson said. "I'll lay you another thousand at that figure, Thornton. What d'you say?"

Thornton's doubt was strong in his face, but his fighting spirit was aroused, the fighting spirit that soars above odds and fails to recognize the impossible. He called Hans and Pete to him. Their sacks were slim, and with his own the three partners could rake together only two hundred dollars. This sum was all they had saved. They laid it unhesitatingly against Matthewson's six hundred.

The team of ten dogs was unhitched, and Buck with his own harness, was put into the sled. He had caught the excitement, and he felt that in some way he must do a great thing for John Thornton. Murmurs of admiration at his splendid appearance went up. He was in perfect condition, without an ounce too much flesh, although he weighed one hundred fifty pounds. His furry coat shone like silk. Down the neck and across the shoulders, his mane, half bristled and seemed to lift with every movement. The great breast and heavy fore-legs went well with the rest of his body, where the muscles showed in tight rolls underneath the skin. Men felt these muscles and proclaimed them hard as iron, and the bets went down to two to one.

"Well, sir!" said a man from the Skookum

Benches. "I offer you eight hundred for him, sir, before the test, sir. Eight hundred just as he stands."

Thornton shook his head and stepped to Buck's side.

"You must stand off from him," Matthewson protested. "Free play and plenty of room."

The crowd fell silent. Thornton knelt down by Buck's side. He took his head in his two hands and rested cheek on cheek. He did not playfully shake him, but he whispered in his ear. "As you love me, Buck. As you love me," was what he whispered. Buck whined with eagerness.

The crowd was watching curiously. The affair was growing mysterious. As Thornton got to his feet, Buck seized his mittened hand between his jaws, pressing in with his teeth and releasing slowly. It was the answer, in terms, not of speech, but of love. Thornton stepped well back.

"Now, Buck," he said.

Buck tightened the harness straps, then slacked them for a matter of several inches. It was the way he had learned.

"Gee!" Thornton's voice rang out, sharp in the tense silence.

Buck swung to the right, ending the movement in a plunge that took up the slack. With a sudden jerk he stopped his one hundred fifty pounds. The load quivered, and from under the runners rose a crisp crackling.

"Haw!" Thornton commanded.

Buck repeated the move, this time to the left. The crackling turned into a snapping, the sled turning and the runners slipping and grating several inches to the side. The sled was broken out. Men were holding their breaths, unconscious of the fact.

"Now, MUSH!"

Thornton's command cracked out like a pistol shot. Buck threw himself forward, tightening the harness with a jarring lunge. His

whole body was gathered compactly together in the tremendous effort, the muscles knotting like live things under the silky fur. His great chest was low to the ground, his head forward and down, while his feet were flying like mad. His claws scarred the hard-packed snow in parallel grooves. The sled swayed and trembled, half-started forward. One of his feet slipped, and one man groaned aloud. Then the sled lurched ahead in rapid jerks, though it never really came to a dead stop again . . . half an inch . . . an inch . . . two inches. The sled gained speed till it was moving steadily along.

Men gasped and began to breathe again, unaware that for a moment they had ceased to breathe. Thornton was running behind, encouraging Buck with short, cheery words.

The distance had been measured off. As he neared the pile of firewood which marked the end of the hundred yards, a cheer began to grow and grow. It burst into a roar as he passed the firewood and halted at command. Every man was tearing himself loose, even Matthewson. Hats and mittens were flying in the air. Men were shaking hands, it did not matter with whom.

But Thornton fell on his knees beside Buck. Head was against head, and he was shaking him back and forth softly and lovingly.

"Now, sir!" spluttered the man from Skookum Bench, "I'll give you a thousand for him, sir, a thousand, sir—twelve hundred, sir."

Thornton rose to his feet. His eyes were wet. The tears were streaming frankly down his cheeks. "Sir," he said, "no, sir."

Buck seized Thornton's hand in his teeth. Thornton shook him back and forth. The onlookers drew back to a respectful distance. Buck had earned sixteen hundred dollars in five minutes for John Thornton. He made it possible for his master to pay off certain debts and to journey with his partners to the east. They were seeking a gold mine, the history of which was as old as the history of the country. Many men had sought it, but few had found it. More than a few had never returned from the search.

This lost mine was steeped in tragedy and covered with mystery. No one knew of the first man who found it. From the beginning there had been an ancient and poorly made cabin. Dying men had sworn to it, and to the mine the site of which it marked. Their stories were of gold nuggets that were unlike any known grade of gold in the Northland.

But no living man had found this treasure, and the dead were dead. John Thornton and Pete and Hans with Buck and half a dozen other dogs went east on an unknown trail. They hoped to achieve where men and dogs as good as themselves had failed. They sledded seventy miles up the Yukon River, swung to the left into the Stewart River. Then they passed the Mayo River and the McQuestion River until the Stewart itself become a streamlet between the peaks which marked the back-bone of the continent.

John Thornton asked little of man or nature. He was unafraid of the wild. With salt and a rifle he could go into the wilderness and live wherever he pleased and as long as he pleased. Being in no haste, he hunted his dinner Indian fashion, in the course of the day's travel. If he failed, he knew that sooner or later he would come to it. So, on this great journey into the east, straight meat was the bill of fare. Tools made up the load on the sled, and time was limitless.

To Buck it was boundless delight, this hunting, fishing, and indefinite wandering through strange places. For weeks at a time they would hold on steadily, day after day, and for weeks they would camp here and there. The dogs would loaf while the men burned holes through frozen muck and gravel. And then washed countless pans of dirt in search of gold by the heat of the fire.

Sometimes they went hungry, sometimes they feasted, all according to the abundance of game and the fortune of hunting. Summer arrived, and dogs and men with packs on their backs rafted across blue mountain lakes. They descended or ascended unknown rivers in slender boats sawed from trees in the standing forest.

The months came and went, and back and forth the men and dogs twisted through the vastness where no men were. Yet where men had been if the Lost Cabin Mine story were true. They went across divides in summer blizzard. They shivered under the midnight sun on bare mountains between the timber line and the endless snows. They dropped into summer valleys amid swarming flies. In the shadows of glaciers, the men picked strawberries and flowers as ripe and fair as any the Southland could boast. In the fall of the year they penetrated a weird lake country, sad and silent, where wild fowl had been. There was

160

no life—only the blowing of chill winds, the forming of ice in sheltered places, and the rippling of waves on lonely beaches.

And through another winter they wandered on the trails of men who had gone before. Once, they came upon a path blazed through the forest, an ancient path, and the Lost Cabin seemed very near. But the path began nowhere and ended nowhere. It remained mystery, as the man who made it and the reason he made it remained mystery. Another time they chanced upon the wreckage of a hunting lodge. Amid the rotted blankets John Thornton found a long-barreled flintlock gun. He knew it for a Hudson's Bay Company gun of the young days in the Northwest. Then such a gun was worth its weight in beaver skins packed flat. And that was all—no hint as to the man who in an early day had built the cabin and left the gun among blankets.

Spring came on once more, and at the end of all their wandering they found, not the Lost

Cabin, but a place in a broad valley. There the gold showed like yellow butter across the bottom of the washing pan. They sought no farther. Each day they worked earned them thousands of dollars in clean dust and nuggets, and they worked every day. The gold was sacked in moose-hide bags, fifty pounds to the bag. They piled it like so much firewood outside the spruce-bough lodge. Like giants they toiled, days flashing on the heels of days like dreams as they heaped the treasure up.

There was nothing for the dogs to do, save the hauling in of meat now and again that Thornton killed. And Buck spent long hours musing by the fire.

14

The Call

The call still sounded in the depths of the forest. It filled him with great unrest and strange desires. It caused him to feel a vague sweet gladness, and he was aware of wild desires and stirrings for he knew not what. Sometimes he pursued the call into the forest, looking for it as though it were a real thing. He barked softly or boldly, as the mood might dictate. He would thrust his nose into the cool wood moss, or into the black soil where long grasses grew. And he would snort with joy at the fat earth smells, or he would crouch for hours. He hid behind trunks of fallen trees, wide-eyed and wide-eared to all that moved and sounded about him. It might be, lying thus, that he hoped to surprise this call he could not understand. But he did not know why he did these various things. He did not reason about them at all.

He would be lying in camp, dozing lazily in the heat of the day, when suddenly his head would lift and his ears cock up, intent and listening. He would spring to his feet and dash away, and on and on, for hours through the forest aisles and across the open spaces where the flowers bunched. He loved to run down dry watercourses, and to creep and spy upon the bird life in the woods. For a day at a time he would lie watching the partridges drumming and strutting up and down. But especially he loved to run in the dim light of the summer midnights, listening to the sounds in the forest. He read signs and sounds as man may read a book, and was seeking for the mysterious something that called. It called waking or sleeping, at all times, for him to come.

One night he sprang from sleep with a start, eager-eyed, nostrils quivering and scenting, his mane bristling. From the forest came the call, distinct and definite as never before. It was a long-drawn howl, like, yet unlike, any noise made by a Husky dog. And he knew it, in the old familiar way, as a sound heard before. He sprang through the sleeping camp and in swift silence dashed through the woods. As he drew closer to the cry he went more slowly, with caution in every movement, till he came to an open place among the trees. Looking out he saw, erect on haunches, with nose pointed to the sky, a long, lean timber wolf.

Buck had made no noise, yet the wolf ceased its howling and tried to sense Buck's presence. He stalked into the open, half crouching, tail straight and stiff, feet falling with care. Every movement showed both threat and friendliness. It was the way that wild beasts meet. But the wolf fled at sight of him. Buck followed, with wild leapings. He ran him into a blind channel, in the bed of the creek, where a timber jam barred the way. The wolf whirled about, snarling and bristling, clipping his teeth together rapidly.

Buck did not attack, but circled him about and hedged him in with friendly advances. The wolf was suspicious and afraid. Buck made three of him in weight, while his head barely reached Buck's shoulder. Watching his chance, he darted away, and the chase was resumed. Time and again he was cornered and the thing repeated. He was in poor condition or Buck could not so easily have overtaken him. He would run till Buck's head was even with his flank. Then he would whirl around at bay, only to dash away again at the first opportunity.

But in the end Buck was rewarded. The wolf, finding that no harm was intended, finally sniffed noses with him. Then they became friendly, and played about in the nervous way of fierce beasts. After some time of this the wolf started off at an easy lope in a manner that plainly showed he was going somewhere. He made it clear to Buck that he was to come. And they ran side by side straight up the creek bed. They came down into a level country where were great stretches of forest and many streams. Through these great stretches they ran steadily, hour after hour, the sun rising higher and the day growing warmer. Buck was wildly glad. He knew he was at last answering the call. He was running by the side of his wood brother toward the place from where the call surely came. Old memories were coming upon him fast. He had done this thing before, somewhere in that other and dimly remembered world.

168

15

Too Late

They stopped by a running stream to drink, and, stopping, Buck remembered John Thornton. He sat down. The wolf started on toward the place from where the call surely came. Then he returned to Buck, sniffing noses and making actions as though to encourage him. But Buck turned about and started slowly on the back track. For the better part of an hour the wild brother ran by his side, whining softly. Then he sat down, pointed his nose upward, and howled. It was a mournful howl. And as Buck held steadily on his way he heard it grow faint and fainter until it was lost in the distance.

John Thornton was eating dinner when Buck dashed into camp and sprang upon him in a frenzy of affection, overturning him. The dog scrambled upon the man licking his face, biting his hand. "Playing the general tomfool," John Thornton called it. He shook Buck back and forth and talked to him lovingly.

For two days and nights Buck never left camp, never let Thornton out of his sight. The dog followed him about at his work, watched him while he ate, saw him into his blankets at night and out of them in the morning. But after two days the call in the forest began to sound louder than ever. Buck's restlessness came back. He remembered the wild brother, the smiling land beyond the divide, and the run through the wide forest stretches. Once again he took to wandering in the woods, but the wild brother came no more. Though he

170

listened through long vigils, the mournful howl was never raised.

He began to sleep out at night, staying away from camp for days at a time. Once he crossed the divide at the head of the creek and went down into the land of timber and streams. There he wandered for a week seeking vainly for fresh sign of the wild brother. He killed his meat as he traveled. And he traveled with the long, easy lope that seemed never to tire him. He fished for salmon in a broad stream that emptied somewhere into the sea, and by this stream he killed a large black bear. It had been blinded by the mosquitoes while fishing, and went raging through the forest helpless and terrible. Even so, it was a hard fight, and it aroused the killer in Buck. And two days later, when he returned to his kill and found a dozen wolverines quarreling over the spoil, he scattered them. Those that fled left two behind who would quarrel no more.

The blood longing became stronger than ever before. He was a killer, a thing that preyed, living on the things that lived, unaided, alone, by his own strength. There was a stray brown streak on his muzzle and above his eyes, and a splash of white hair that ran down his chest. Otherwise he might well have been mistaken for a gigantic wolf, larger than the largest of the breed. He had the St. Bernard size and weight, but it was his shepherd mother who had given shape to that size and weight. His muzzle was the long wolf muzzle of any wolf. And his head, somewhat broader, was the wolf head on a massive scale. His muscles snapped into play sharply, like springs. His cunning was wolf cunning, and wild cunning. His intelligence was shepherd intelligence and St. Bernard intelligence. And all this, plus an experience gained in the fiercest of schools, made him as savage as any beast.

"There never was such a dog," said John Thornton one day, as the partners watched

172

Buck marching out of camp. They did not see the instant and terrible change which took place as soon as he was within the forest. He no longer marched. At once he became a thing of the wild, stealing along softly, cat-footed. He was a passing shadow that appeared and disappeared among the shadows. He knew how to take advantage of every cover, to crawl on his belly like a snake, or to leap and strike.

He could take a bird from its nest, kill a rabbit as it slept. He could snap in midair the little chipmunks fleeing a second too late for the trees. Fish, in open pools, were not too quick for him, nor were beaver, mending their dams. He killed to eat, because he preferred to eat what he killed himself. A lurking humor ran through his deeds. It was his delight to steal upon the squirrels. When he all but had them, he let them go, chattering in mortal fear to the treetops.

As the fall of the year came on, the moose appeared in greater number. They moved slowly down to meet the winter in the lower and warmer valleys. Buck had already dragged down a stray part-grown moose calf. He wished strongly for a larger one and came upon it one day on the divide at the head of the creek. A band of twenty moose had crossed over from the land of streams and timber. Chief among them was a great bull. He was in a savage temper and stood over six feet from the ground. Back and forth the bull tossed his great antlers, which branched to fourteen points and were seven feet within the tips. His small eyes burned with a vicious and bitter light, while he roared with fury at sight of Buck.

From the bull's side, a feathered arrow end stuck out which accounted for his savageness. Guided by instinct Buck proceeded to cut the bull out from the herd. It was no slight task. He would bark and dance about in front of the bull, just out of reach of the great antlers. The terrible splay hoofs could have stamped

174

his life out with a single blow. Unable to turn his back on the fanged danger and go on, the bull would be driven into a rage. At such moments he charged Buck, who retreated craftily. As soon as he was thus separated from his fellows, two or three of the younger bulls would charge back upon Buck. Then the wounded bull could rejoin the herd.

There is a patience of the wild that holds motionless for endless hours the spider in its web and the snake in its coils. This patience belongs peculiarly to life when it hunts its living food. It belonged to Buck as he clung to the herd, stopping its march and irritating the young bulls. For half a day he worried the cows with their half-grown calves, and drove the wounded bull mad with helpless rage. Buck attacked from all sides, cutting out his victim as fast as it could rejoin its mates, and wearing out their patience.

The day ended and the sun finally dropped to its bed in the northwest. The young bulls retraced their steps more and more unwillingly to the aid of their leader. The downcoming winter was hurrying them on to the lower levels. But it seemed they could never shake off this tireless creature that held them back. Besides, it was not the life of the herd, or of the young bulls, that was threatened. The life of only one member was demanded, and in the end they were content to pay the toll.

As darkness fell the old bull stood with lowered head, watching the cows, the calves, and the young bulls. They shambled on at a rapid pace through the fading light. He could not follow, for before his nose leaped the merciless fanged terror that would not let him go. He had lived a long, strong life, full of fight and struggle. At the end he faced death at the teeth of a creature whose head did not reach beyond his knees.

From then on, night and day, Buck never left his prey. He never gave it a moment's rest, never permitted it to browse the leaves of trees or the shoots of young birch and willow. Nor did he give the wounded bull opportunity to drink in the slender trickling streams they crossed. Often the bull burst into long stretches of flight. At such times Buck did not attempt to stay him, but loped easily at his heels. He was satisfied with the way the game was played. Buck lay down when the moose stood still, but attacked him fiercely when he tried to eat or drink.

The great head drooped more and more under its trees of horns, and the trot grew weaker and weaker. The bull took to standing for long periods, with nose to the ground and ears drooping limply. And Buck found more time in which to get water for himself and in which to rest.

At such moments, he panted with red lolling tongue and with eyes fixed upon the big bull. It appeared to Buck that a change was coming over the face of things. He could feel a new stir in the land. As the moose were coming into the land, other kinds of life were coming in. Forest and stream and air seemed alive with their presence. The news of it was borne in upon him, not by sight, or sound, or smell, but by some other and subtler sense. He heard nothing, saw nothing, yet he knew that the land was somehow different. He resolved to find out after he had finished the business in hand.

At last, at the end of the fourth day, he pulled the great moose down. For a day and a night he remained by the kill, eating and sleeping, turn and turn about. Then, rested, refreshed and strong, he turned his face toward camp and John Thornton. He broke into the long easy lope, and went on, hour after hour, never at loss for the way. He headed straight home through strange country more sure of his direction than any man with his magnetic needle.

As he held on he became more and more

conscious of the new stir in the land. There was life abroad in it different from the life which had been there throughout the summer. No longer was this fact subtle and mysterious. The birds talked of it, the squirrels chattered about it, the very breeze whispered of it. Several times he stopped and drew in the fresh morning air in great sniffs. He could read a message which made him leap on with greater speed. He was oppressed with a sense of disaster happening, if it had not already happened. As he crossed the last watershed and dropped down into the valley toward camp, he proceeded with greater caution.

Three miles away he came upon a fresh trail that sent his neck hair rippling and bristling. It led straight toward camp and John Thornton. Buck hurried on, every nerve straining and tense, alert to the details which told a story—all but the end. His nose gave him a varying description of the passage of the life on the heels of which he was traveling.

He noticed the silence of the forest. The bird life had flitted. The squirrels were in hiding.

As Buck slid along, his nose was jerked suddenly to the side as though a positive force had gripped and pulled it. He followed the new scent into a thicket and found Nig. He was lying on his side, dead where he had dragged himself, an arrow sticking out from either side of his body.

A hundred yards farther on, Buck came upon one of the sled dogs Thornton had bought in Dawson. This dog was thrashing about in a death struggle, directly on the trail, and Buck passed around him without stopping.

From Thornton's camp came the faint sound of many voices, rising and falling in a sing song chant. Bellying forward to the edge of the clearing, he found Hans, lying on his face, feathered with arrows like a porcupine. At the same instant Buck peered out where the spruce-bough cabin had been and saw what made his hair leap straight up on his neck and shoulders.

Overpowering rage swept over him. He did not know that he growled, but he growled aloud with a terrible ferocity. For the last time in his life, because of his great love for John Thornton, he lost his head.

The Yeehat Indians were dancing about the wreckage of the spruce-bough cabin.

The Yeehats heard a fearful roaring and saw rushing upon them an animal the like of which they had never seen before. It was Buck, a live hurricane of fury, hurling himself upon them in a frenzy to destroy. Buck sprang at the chief of the Yeehats, ripping his throat wide open till the jugular spouted a fountain of blood. Then with the next bound he tore wide the throat of a second man. There was no withstanding him. He plunged about in their very midst, tearing, rending, destroying. In constant and terrific motion he defied the arrows they discharged at him. In fact, so rapid were his movements, and so closely were the Indians tangled together that they shot one another with the arrows. One young hunter hurled a spear at Buck in midair. It went through the chest of another hunter with such force that the point broke through the skin of the back and stood out beyond. Then a panic seized the Yeehats, and they fled in terror to the woods, yelling as they fled that it was the Evil Spirit.

And truly Buck was the Fiend raging at their heels and dragging them down like deer as they raced through the trees. It was a fateful day for the Yeehats. They scattered far and wide over the country. It was not till a week later that the last of them gathered together in a lower valley and counted their losses.

As for Buck, he returned to the camp and found Pete where he had been killed in his blankets in the first moment of surprise. Thornton's desperate struggle was fresh-writ-

ten on the earth. And Buck scented every detail of it down to the edge of a deep pool. By the edge, head and forefeet in the water, lay Skeet, faithful to the last. The pool itself, muddy and discolored hid what it contained, and it contained John Thornton. Buck followed his tracks into the water, from which no track led away.

All day Buck brooded by the pool or roamed restlessly about the camp. Death, he knew, and he knew John Thornton was dead. It left a great void in him, like hunger, but a void which ached and ached, and which food could not fill. At times, when he paused to look at the carcasses of the Yeehats, he forgot the pain of it. And at such times he was aware of a great pride in himself,—a pride greater than any he had yet experienced. He had killed man, the noblest game of all. And he had killed in the face of the law of club and fang. He sniffed the bodies curiously. They had died so easily. It was harder to kill a

Husky dog than them. They were no match at all, were it not for their arrows and spears and clubs. Thenceforward he would be unafraid of them except when they bore in their hands their arrows, spears, and clubs.

Night came on, and a full moon rose high over the trees. He stood up, listening and scenting. From far away drifted a faint, sharp yelp, followed by a chorus of similar sharp yelps. As the moments passed, the yelps grew closer and louder. Buck walked to the center of the open space and listened. It was the call. As never before, he was ready to obey. John Thornton was dead. The last tie was broken. Man and the claims of man no longer bound him.

The wolves hunted their living meat, as the Yeehats were hunting it, on the flanks of the moose. At last the wolves had crossed over from the land of streams and timber and invaded Buck's valley. Into the clearing where the moonlight streamed, they poured in a silvery flood. In the center of the clearing stood Buck, motionless as a statue, waiting their coming. They were awed, so still and large he stood. A moment's pause fell, till the boldest one leaped straight for him. Like a flash Buck struck and he had such marvelous quickness that he turned on his hind legs, snapped and gashed and was everywhere at once. He presented a front which was apparently unbroken so swiftly did he whirl and guard from side to side. But to prevent them from getting behind him, he went backwards down past the pool and into the creek bed. Finally he brought up against a high gravel bank. He worked along to a corner in the bank which the men had made in the course of mining. He was protected on three sides with nothing to do but face the front.

And so well did he face it, that at the end of half an hour the wolves drew back. The tongues of all were out and lolling, the white fangs showing cruelly white in the moonlight.

Some were lying down with heads raised and ears pricked forward. Others stood on their feet, watching him. Still others were lapping water from the pool. One wolf, long and lean and gray, advanced cautiously, in a friendly manner. And Buck recognized the wild brother with whom he had run for a night and a day. He was whining softly, and, as Buck whined, they touched noses.

Then an old wolf, gaunt and battle-scarred, came forward. Buck began to snarl, but sniffed noses with him. Whereupon the old wolf sat down, pointed nose at the moon, and broke out the long wolf howl. The others sat down and howled. And now the call came to Buck unmistakably. He, too, sat down and howled. The pack crowded around him, snffiing.

The leaders of the pack sprang away into the woods. The wolves swung in behind, yelping in chorus. And Buck ran with them, side by side with his wild brother, yelping as he ran.

ABOUT THIS BOOK

A great, gloriously coated wolf, like, and yet unlike all other wolves comes every summer to a certain valley where the Yeehat Indians are afraid to go. Here a yellow stream flows from the rotted moose-hide sacks and sinks into the ground. Long grasses grow through it hiding its yellow from the sun. Here he muses for a time howling once long and mournfully, before he departs.

Thus Jack London ends his famous story about Judge Miller's pampered pet BUCK who left California to set foot on his first snow on the Dyea Beach in our forty-ninth state, Alaska.

Author of fifty books, John Griffith London was probably best known for THE CALL OF THE WILD which sold almost a million and a half copies. By 1913 he was said to be the best known, highest paid, and most popular writer of all time. He practically educated himself after he discovered the library in Oakland, California at the age of ten.

Extreme poverty prevented his entering high school until the age of nineteen and also prevented him from attending the University of California for more than one year. Sometimes as a child he worked a ten-hour day for only ten cents an hour, but before his death at the age of forty he had earned by his writing and also had spent a million dollars.

Mary Yost Sandrus has edited THE CALL OF THE WILD to retain the entire narrative and preserve the original London style. A little was cut for space and to sustain the pace of the story.

Since more than 95% of the vocabulary in this story may be found in the first thousand words that most people learn as Thorndike lists them in A TEACHER'S WORD BOOK, it is at the reading level of anyone with minimum reading skills.

The books in this series provide easy reading material for students, regardless of their proficiency in reading:

SIX GREAT STORIES	HUCKLEBERRY FINN
TREASURE ISLAND	AROUND THE WORLD IN EIGHTY DAYS
WHEN WASHINGTON DANCED	CAPTAINS COURAGEOUS
LORNA DOONE	THE YEARS BETWEEN
MOBY DICK	20,000 LEAGUES UNDER THE SEA
TOM SAWYER	FAMOUS MYSTERIES
THE LAST OF THE MOHICANS	IN OTHER DAYS
SILAS MARNER	THE PRINCE AND THE PAUPER
DAVID COPPERFIELD	ADVENTURES WITH ANIMALS
ROBINSON CRUSOE	THE CALL OF THE WILD
EIGHT TREASURED STORIES	PEOPLE TO REMEMBER
JULIUS CAESAR in Modern English	TOP FLIGHT
MACBETH in Modern English	ON TARGET

The following original stories, translations, or retold stories have a high interest level to appeal to boys and girls with minimum reading skills:

THE BOXCAR CHILDREN	HIDDEN SILVER
SURPRISE ISLAND	1001 NIGHTS
THE SIX ROBBENS	THE YELLOW HOUSE MYSTERY
THE FLYING TRUNK	MYSTERY RANCH
THE MYSTERY OF	MIKE'S MYSTERY
EDISON BROWN	BLUE BAY MYSTERY

Busy Baby
+
Cindy Rogers